For Class 2, Stockland C of E Primary Academy

Contents

THE WHIZZ POP CHOCOLATE SHOP

KATE SAUNDERS

A YEARLING BOOK

Text copyright © 2012 by Kate Saunders
Cover art copyright © 2013 by Tyson Mangelsdorf

All rights reserved. Published in the United States by Yearling, an imprint of Random House Children's Books, a division of Random House LLC, a Penguin Random House Company, New York. Originally published in paperback in the United Kingdom by Scholastic Ltd., London, in 2012, and subsequently published in hardcover in the United States by Delacorte Press, an imprint of Random House Children's Books, New York, in 2013.

Yearling and the jumping horse design are registered trademarks of Random House LLC.

Visit us on the Web! randomhousekids.com
Educators and librarians, for a variety of teaching tools, visit us at
RHTeachersLibrarians.com

The Library of Congress has cataloged the hardcover edition of this work as follows:
Saunders, Kate.
The Whizz Pop Chocolate Shop / Kate Saunders. — 1st ed.   p. cm.
Summary: Eleven-year-old twins Oz and Lily are recruited by a talking cat to assist her and MI6 in foiling the dastardly plans of their great-great-uncle, a chocolatier who used magic to make a candy that bestows immortality.
ISBN 978-0-385-74301-3 (hc) — ISBN 978-0-375-99090-8 (lib. bdg.) —
ISBN 978-0-307-98034-2 (ebook)
[1. Magic—Fiction. 2. Adventure and adventurers—Fiction. 3. Immortality—Fiction. 4. Cats—Fiction. 5. Brothers and sisters—Fiction. 6. Twins—Fiction. 7. London (England)—Fiction. 8. England—Fiction.]   I. Title.
PZ7.S2539Whi 2013   [Fic]—dc23   2011053081

ISBN 978-0-385-74302-0 (pbk.)
Printed in the United States of America
10 9 8 7

First Yearling Edition 2014

Random House Children's Books supports the First Amendment and celebrates the right to read.

1

Skittle Street

"We'll probably sell the place," Dad said, from the driver's seat. "I shouldn't think it's worth much. The letter said it had been empty for more than seventy years."

"It's probably a rat-infested ruin," said Oz.

"Rats!" squeaked Lily. "I hate rats!"

"Keep your wig on, Lil," Dad said over his shoulder. "We're only taking one quick look. I've never inherited a house before."

The previous day, a strange parcel had arrived at the Spoffard family's small house in Washford Common. It was from a solicitor named Mr. Spike. In his letter, he explained that Dad's great-uncle Pierre had died and left him a house. The parcel had also contained a set of old keys and the title deeds to 18 Skittle Street, London N7.

At first Bruce Spoffard had thought it must be a mistake. As far as he knew, his great-uncle Pierre had been dead since long before he was born. "The three

Spoffard brothers—my great-grandfather and two great-uncles—were killed in a freak accident in 1938, when the tram they were in ran off the Thames Embankment."

"Pierre obviously didn't die on that tram," said Oz. "I bet he deliberately faked his own death. Maybe his brothers did too."

"Steady on," Dad said, smiling. "Even if they did, they wouldn't have lasted until now—they'd be about a hundred and twenty!"

"I'm sure there's a perfectly simple explanation," Mum said. "Whatever it is, this house couldn't have come along at a better time—what with the mortgage and the twins' shoes, and Oz's music lessons and Lily's tutor, and a new baby on the way."

"I don't want a tutor," said Lily. "Sandra's a cow— she blames me when I can't do things."

Her parents had heard this complaint many times before, and now ignored it. They had an amazing talent for not hearing things they didn't like.

"And this old car's on the point of conking out," Dad added.

"It's a shame you had such expensive kids," Lily said crossly. "Oz costs a lot because he's a genius, and I do because I'm stupid."

"For the last time," Mum said, studying the street map, "you are not stupid. You have dyslexia."

"I'm not a genius, either," said Oz. "If I were a genius I wouldn't need music lessons, would I?"

Neither parent was really listening. "Where are we, anyway?" Mum asked. "I don't know this part of London at all."

"We're just coming into Holloway," Dad said. "Not long now."

Bruce Spoffard was a tall, bony man with curly black hair cut very short around his bald patch and a kindly, rather sleepy-looking face. His wife, Emily, was a small, pale person with straight blond hair and a sweet, far-away smile. Their eleven-year-old twins, Oz (short for Oscar) and Lily, were an interesting mixture of them both. Oz had straight light-brown hair and greenish-blue eyes. Lily had crazy curly black hair, a pale face dotted with freckles and eyes like black buttons.

Lily stared out of the window. Despite the bright sunshine, this section of London was gray and dreary, a hot mess of noisy roads and run-down shops. Washford Common had trees and gardens; here she couldn't see a single leaf or blade of grass.

"Here we are—this is Skittle Street."

Dad turned the car onto a short street with a large block of flats down all one side. On the other side was a row of sooty, shabby Victorian shops. In silence, they all got out of the car and stared at the shops.

Oz's interest quickened. He hadn't cared that much

about seeing the new house, but he thought there was something quite intriguing about this street.

The shop at the end of the row was boarded up and covered with graffiti. But the supermarket next door had a colorful display of fruit and vegetables spilling out onto the pavement, and window boxes of scarlet geraniums on the upstairs sills. The hardware shop next to it had bouquets of rainbow-colored feather dusters hanging in the doorway. Next to this was a very cheerful-looking cafe, its steamy windows filled with pictures advertising all-day breakfasts.

Across the road, a black boy of about Oz's age was skateboarding on the concrete ramp that led down to the dustbins. Every time he got to the bottom of the ramp he did a showy corkscrew twist—the kind Oz could never do himself without falling off. He thought how brilliant it would be to have a friend like this boy, though he was probably too cool to be friends with a violin-playing nerd like Oz. The boys in his class mostly treated him as if he were invisible.

"Well, this is my new house," Dad said, in front of the boarded-up shop.

Under the crust of dirt, you could just make out the curly letters above the door.

Lily nudged Oz. "What does that say?"

" 'Spoffard Bros.,' " Oz read to her (Lily's dyslexia made reading difficult, especially when the letters had funny shapes). "Established 1927—hey, Dad, this was your family business!"

"Yes," Dad said, "and I can remember my grandmother telling me about it when I was little. You know the story. They were makers of fine chocolate. They had a showroom in Piccadilly, but this was their workshop, and Great-Uncle Pierre lived upstairs." He began to search through the bunch of keys. "I assumed it had been sold years ago; funny that it's been here all this time, empty."

"Should we risk going inside?" Mum wondered. "It might not be safe."

Something soft brushed Lily's foot. It was a cat—a rather stout but very beautiful female cat, with long golden-brown fur and bright, solemn green eyes of a peculiar square shape. She sat down on the pavement and stared at Lily.

"Hello," whispered Lily. She longed for a cat and had asked for one for their eleventh birthday two months ago, but her parents had said that cats and new babies didn't mix. She bent down to stroke the cat's soft, smooth head.

"Lily," Mum said, "what on earth are you doing?"

"Look—isn't this cat adorable?"

"Darling, what are you burbling about now?"

"I'm not burbling!" Lily looked down at the cat. She had gone. There was no sign of her.

"Oz, you saw that cat, didn't you?"

"No." Oz had been watching the skateboarding boy.

"She must've run away when she sensed hostility."

Mum groaned. "Please let's not have the cat argument now."

"Found it!" cried Dad. He unlocked the front door, cautiously pushing it open. It opened onto a dark passage with a door at the other end and another door in the left-hand wall.

Lily had expected a smell of dampness and decay, yet the air was filled with a wistful, dusty sweetness.

"It still smells of chocolate," Oz said. "You wouldn't think a smell could last that long."

Dad patted the door on the left. "I'm guessing this was the workshop, on the ground floor. And this will be the residential part of the house," he said, opening the door at the end of the passage.

The Spoffards walked into a space filled with sunlight. The first thing they saw was the only object in the empty, dusty, echoing house—a huge, hand-colored photograph hanging on the wall, of a fat man with a mustache holding a cat.

It was the same cat Lily had seen outside, she was sure of it: those were the same strange, narrow eyes, green and hard as chips of emerald; the same tartan collar and silver bell.

"Good grief," said Dad. "I think that's my great-uncle Pierre."

Oz read the writing underneath the picture. " 'Pierre and Demerara, 1929.' "

"Demerara—that's an odd name for a cat," said Mum. "He must have named her after demerara sugar. She's the same sort of color. Wow—Bruce, look at the size of this place!"

She had lost interest in the cat, craning her neck to look up the staircase.

Lily moved closer to the picture. The cat in Pierre's arms couldn't be the same cat she had stroked outside—but she couldn't shake off the feeling that it had been Demerara. Did cats have ghosts?

The house part of 18 Skittle Street was big—very big, compared to their tiny three-bedroom row house in Washford Common. On the upper floors were a sitting room and six bedrooms. On the ground floor, behind the workshop, was a large kitchen with an antique stove, and an overgrown, weedy yard.

Bruce and Emily Spoffard started trooping up and down the stairs, measuring the rooms and calling excitedly to each other.

"Bruce—there's a lovely room for us, with a room next door for the baby!"

"Emily—the yard is gigantic!"

Lily quickly got bored with looking at an empty

house and returned to the hall to gaze at the picture of Demerara.

Oz came down the stairs to join her. "I thought they were going to sell this place. Now they're talking as if they want to live here."

"I don't think I'd mind." Lily was still looking at Demerara. "Would you?"

"I'd like it," said Oz. "It would be great to live in a house as big as this, and it's a lot closer to my music lessons—I wouldn't have to spend half my time on trains. And the yard's big enough for a basketball hoop." He'd wanted one for his birthday, but there hadn't been anywhere to put it in their yard in Washford Common.

"But I feel a stirring at the marrow of my bones," Lily said. "There's something weird about this place."

"You think something's weird everywhere."

"Don't pretend you don't feel it too."

"It's a strange old house, that's all," Oz said. "Do you want them to send us back into therapy?"

Lily was cross. "That was when we were two. You know this is different. Did you really not see that cat outside?"

"No."

"I'm going to look at the workshop." Lily went out into the passage and tried the door of the workshop, where the Spoffard Brothers had made their chocolate.

It was not locked, so very cautiously, she pushed it open a few centimeters. "Maybe we shouldn't."

"We're here now." Oz pushed her aside, taking a step into the confusion of black and gray shadows. He spotted a light switch on the wall and flipped it, and the room sprang shockingly to life.

For a long moment, Oz and Lily gazed in silence.

"This is fantastic," said Oz.

Lily murmured, "This is—magic."

For a long moment they stood in silence, gazing around a large room that looked like a dusty cave crammed with extraordinary objects. It was dominated by a large, deep fireplace with a grill like a barbecue. A big metal cylinder, festooned with cobwebs, loomed in one corner and in the middle of the room was a long bench with a marble top. On top of this stood a flat, smooth stone with an ashy grate underneath it. Saucepans of every size, from an egg cup to a small boat, hung on the walls and from the ceiling. One wall was taken up by an immense rack of knives and tools, and there was a stack of shelves piled high with hollow metal shapes.

"I thought it would be more like a sort of kitchen," Oz said. He went over to the tools and picked up a silver knife with a rounded blade.

Lily blew the dust off a large metal shape about twenty-five centimeters long. It was shaped like half a

Father Christmas, carrying half a sack of toys. "Oh, I get it—it's a chocolate mold—see? Here's the other half for the other side. You line it with chocolate, and when it gets hard you stick them together to make a whole one."

Oz stopped fingering the oddly shaped knives and came over. "These bowl things are molds for Easter eggs—the biggest is huge." He touched the side of it with one finger and wrote "OZ" in the dust. "Imagine getting an egg this big—it'd last you the whole summer!"

Lily held up the two halves of the Father Christmas mold. "Isn't this beautiful? I don't think I could bear to eat it."

"Kids!" Dad yelled, somewhere above them. "Come here a minute!"

They left the workshop, remembering to switch off the light.

"Funny that the electricity's still on," Oz said. "I wonder who's been paying the bills."

Their parents were in the empty sitting room upstairs.

"We've made a big decision," Dad said excitedly. "We've decided to sell the house in Washford Common and move here."

"It's in amazingly good condition." Mum's eyes shone. "And this is the perfect time to move, with you two about to change schools, and the baby coming."

"And it's only a short bus ride to college," Dad said (he worked at a college in the middle of the city). "I know the old saying that there's no such thing as a free lunch, but this house is looking better every minute."

"Of course, it will mean a bit of an upheaval," Mum said. "Lily, I'm afraid we can't travel all the way to Sandra's every week. We'll have to find you a new tutor."

"What—we can fire Sandra?" Lily cried joyfully. "When?"

"Not so fast," said Dad. "Are you two absolutely sure you like this house?"

"It's great," Oz said. "Can I have a basketball hoop?"

"I think it's wonderful," said Lily. "I'm pretty sure it's haunted, and I've always wanted to live in a haunted house."

"Of course it's not haunted!" Dad folded his arms, a sign that he was about to say something important. "This is a family that does NOT believe in ghosts! If I hear one more word about ghosts or ghouls or long-legged beasties, we're going straight back to Washford Common—is that clear, Miss Nutella?" (Nutella was his nickname for Lily when he thought she was being particularly nutty.)

Lily shrugged. "Suit yourself. At least I tried to warn you."

That night, Lily's bedtime rituals took longer than usual.

No matter how tired she was, there were certain things she always had to do.

She took off her clothes, folding them neatly and placing them on the chair beside the desk, and proceeded to put on her pajamas; then she took the bed toys off the bed and put them on the desk with the desk toys. She didn't like walking between the light switch and the bed in the dark, so she made stepping-stones across the floor with old picture books and annuals. She adjusted the funny little net that was supposed to catch bad dreams (it didn't work). Finally, she switched off the overhead light. She had hung up six strings of colored fairy lights (Dad fretted that they would burn the house down, and sometimes crept into her bedroom and switched them off when she was asleep, which made her furious), and the little room was bathed in their magical glow.

In the tiny bedroom next door, Oz was playing his violin. The wall was paper-thin, but Lily didn't mind the constant music. He played very well, and the sound made her feel safe and peaceful, as if she were hearing a sweet voice she had heard before she was born.

She would miss this bedroom. It was stuffed from floor to ceiling with toys, clothes, paints, books and makeup, and every single object was arranged with extreme neatness. Lily was famously fussy about her bedroom. All her old soft toys were strictly arranged according to color and size. Her colored pens and pencils lay in neat rows in their original boxes and her collection of makeup was set out across the top of the chest of drawers.

But I don't mind leaving, she thought—not if I can see Demerara again. If they won't let me have a real cat, a ghost cat has got to be the next best thing.

She fell asleep thinking about Demerara, and had a ridiculous dream about that magnificent cat being caught in the dream catcher and shouting, "What is this LOATHSOME contraption?"

2

The Haunted
Chocolate Shop

The Spoffards moved into 18 Skittle Street in the
third week of the summer holidays. Once most of
the beds, chairs, tables and boxes of clutter had been
put in the right rooms, Bruce Spoffard told his children
to sort out their new bedrooms.

For Oz, this was an easy matter. He put his duvet on
the bed (it looked very small in this big room), set up
his desk, computer and music stand and left everything
else inside the boxes—he wanted plenty of floor space
for the giant toy car track he was planning.

In the room next door, Lily was in one of her states.

"It's too big!" Oz heard her wailing. "My things don't
look right anymore! The wallpaper's staring at me!"

Oz sighed to himself; poor old Lily, she hated
change.

Mum was trying to comfort her. "Darling, don't be
silly," Oz heard her say. "How can yellow roses stare at
you?"

"They look like evil faces!"

14

"Lily, do get a grip—moving house is stressful for everyone. You'll soon settle down."

Oz decided not to get involved. He went downstairs to help Dad with the towering heaps of cardboard boxes on the pavement.

"Blimey, who knew we had so much stuff?" Dad groaned. "It's incredible our old house didn't explode! Oz—take all the boxes with question marks on them into the workshop, until I've figured out what to do with them."

Oz used one of the boxes to prop open the workshop door and switched on the light.

Something moved on the floor. Oz's heart jumped with shock.

It was a thin, dirty, gray-brown rat.

Oz wasn't too scared of rats in general, but this rat was different—it was smoking. It sat on its haunches with the stub of a cigarette clutched in one skinny paw while its mouth, with its horrid single fang, puffed out a cloud of disgusting smoke.

This is not normal, Oz thought dazedly.

The rat stared at Oz. It suddenly let out a series of squeaks—"Ugh! Ugh! Ugh!"—which were just like a particularly revolting smoker's cough—and bolted out the workshop door.

Oz put down the box he was holding and took a deep breath. Lily kept saying this house was weird, but she thought all sorts of places were weird, so he hadn't really listened to her. A smoking rat, however, was weird in anybody's book. What should he do?

If he told his parents, would they believe him? Probably not, he decided—especially if he told them about the smoking. He didn't know much about the habits of rats, but he was pretty sure they didn't smoke. If he told Lily—who hated both rats and smoking—she would go berserk.

I might have imagined it, he thought; it'll be a lot easier if I pretend it didn't happen; no, of course it didn't happen.

But there was a lingering smell of old smoke, and when Oz went back into the street to fetch more boxes, he saw a crumpled cigarette end smoldering beside the drain.

When the moving van had gone and Lily had stopped crying, Dad went to the cafe and bought fish and chips for supper, which they ate at the kitchen table.

"It looks tiny in this big kitchen," Mum said. "We'll have to get a bigger one."

"No!" Lily blurted out. "I want this one—this table is a bit of home!"

Her parents looked at each other wearily.

"You haven't lost your home," Mum said. "You've only moved to a new one."

"It smells all wrong."

"Come on, Nutella," said Dad. "Your wallpaper will soon stop plotting against you."

"Stop it, Bruce," Mum said. "Teasing her won't help. We've come to an agreement. Lily's going to have the picture of Pierre in her bedroom."

"Great," said Dad, his mouth full of chips, "I was wondering what to do with that ugly thing."

He and Oz had managed to set up the television in the upstairs sitting room, and after supper, everyone except Lily settled down to watch *Dr. Who*. Lily went back to working in the scary, rose-infested chaos of her room. This was not home. It couldn't be anything like home until the bags and boxes were unpacked and the soft toys set out in tidy, color-coded rows on the shelves. She wouldn't have agreed to sleep here at all if Mum hadn't given her the picture of Pierre and his cat.

Lily kept glancing at it while she worked. Great-Great-Uncle Pierre looked very kind, she thought; he was smiling, and his black mustache twirled up at the ends like another smile. And Demerara looked as sweet as the golden-brown sugar she was named after.

By the time Mum (and then Dad) had told her to go to bed, the room was a little less strange and chaotic. Lily put on her pajamas, moved the bed toys and switched off the glaring overhead light and bedside lamp. The glow of the six strings of fairy lights went nowhere in this big space—but at least she couldn't see the nasty roses.

She lay awake for a long time, eventually drifting into a kind of half-sleep—and then jolted awake to the sound of whispering.

"Great lump of a girl!"

"Doesn't she look stupid?"

"I can't stand those pajamas."

"They look awful with that hair."

"If that was MY hair I'd cut it off."

The spiteful yellow roses were saying mean things about her, like the mean girls at school who tittered at her when she didn't understand things. Lily lay very still under her duvet, rigid with terror, unable to scream.

Suddenly, a long shadow fell across the floor.

"Demerara!" choked Lily. She sat up and switched on her bedside lamp. There, standing in the middle of the rug, was the mysterious golden-brown cat. And of course it was the original Demerara—she was identical to the cat in the photograph.

Lily was so captivated by the sight of her that it took her a moment to notice the whispering had stopped.

Demerara gazed around scornfully. Quick as lightning, she pounced at the wall near Lily's bed. Her long claws gleamed like razor blades. She scratched at one of the yellow roses; to Lily's amazement, it seemed to lift right off the wall, leaving a blank white space where it had been. The yellow petals hung in rags from Demerara's claws, and then she tossed them into her mouth.

"Wow," Lily said. "Now I know this is a dream."

"Hmmm—musty," said Demerara.

This was a brilliant dream. The cat was talking to her. Lily nearly laughed aloud. "Hello."

"Oh, you can hear me, can you? Thank goodness—I thought I'd never get it right. I tried jumping into your dream, but I got caught in that awful net thing. Welcome to Skittle Street."

Lily sat up properly and got out of bed. "Are you a ghost?"

"Certainly not," said Demerara. "Don't worry about those roses, by the way—they won't be giving you any more trouble."

"How do you know?"

"It was merely a question of finding and eating the ringleader. This room has been empty for too long, and the roses started to turn bad. That's the trouble with leftover magic."

Lily was so entranced by the sight and sound of a cat talking that she could hardly pay attention to what Demerara was saying. It was fascinating to watch a cat's mouth moving in speech, and her voice was an extraordinary sort of breathy yowling. Lily looked at the wallpaper. The roses were just the same, yet she sensed the change in the atmosphere, like a garden after a storm. This was a really five-star, big-budget dream.

"How does your wallpaper feel now?" Demerara asked.

"Sulky," said Lily.

"That won't last." The cat raised her golden head. "I love what you've done with this room, by the way."

"Thanks."

"You have such gorgeous things—may I have a little peek?"

"Go ahead."

In two graceful leaps, Demerara jumped onto the small chest of drawers, where Lily kept her collection of makeup. Though she never wore makeup, she loved her lipsticks and blushers and pots of body glitter.

Demerara delicately touched the neat row of lipsticks with her little paw. "Lily, I know this is pushy—but could I have one of your lipsticks? I've always wanted one."

"Well—OK." Lily didn't think cats had lips but wanted to be generous. "Help yourself."

"Oh, thank you! And could you read the names?"

"I can't actually read them, because I'm dyslexic and the writing's too tiny," Lily said. "But I got Oz to read them for me and now I know them by heart."

"And could you open them so I can see the colors?"

Lily went over to the chest of drawers and began

the strange process of showing lipsticks to a cat. "This one's called Cheeky Plum—this is Apricot Sunset—Red Rascal—"

Demerara took a while to make up her mind, but eventually chose Pink Limit.

"Thank you, Lily, it's divine. I do like bright colors."

"Er—what shall I do with it?" Cats didn't have handbags, after all.

Demerara smiled and said purrily, "I'll leave it here and collect it later. We really should be getting on."

"Getting on with what?"

"We have to wake up Oz."

"What—really?"

"Lily, dear," Demerara said patiently, "I thought you'd gotten it by now—this isn't a dream."

3

Demerara's Flat

In the warm, dark depths of his deep sleep, someone was shaking his shoulder.

"Oz—wake up!"

"Go away."

"Oz, you have to wake up NOW," Lily hissed in his ear. "This is an emergency!"

Oz shook the fog out of his head. "Why don't you wake Mum and Dad?"

"It's not that sort of emergency," Lily whispered. "Keep your voice down—Demerara's here, and she can talk and she wants us to come down to the workshop—"

"You woke me up because of that imaginary cat?"

A strange, shivery voice said, "I am NOT imaginary."

There she was on his floor, the golden-brown cat with narrow green eyes, exactly like the cat in the photograph. He sat up quickly, his heart hammering.

"Do calm down," said Demerara. "You'll only hold me up if you refuse to believe your senses, and I have a lot of business to get through."

"Wh-what?" said Oz.

"I called you to this house for a reason."

It was amazingly odd to be talking to a cat. "You didn't call us here," Oz said feebly. "It was a lawyer, Mr. Spike."

"Oh, yes—Mr. Spike!" Demerara's green eyes narrowed and Oz realized she was laughing. "You could say he works for me. Now put some slippers on and come downstairs."

Oz was scared, but also incredibly curious. He had no idea where his slippers were, so he stuffed his feet into his sneakers. As quietly as possible, he and Lily crept out of the room after the silent cat. The stairs creaked, and it was hard to be quiet in a new house when you didn't know where to put your feet, but they managed to get to the workshop without waking their parents.

"Put the light on, please," Demerara's peculiar voice said, in the shadows. "Let's take a proper look at each other."

Oz switched on the light. He'd been assuming that this cat would look misty and spooky, but she was solid and stout, and if she hadn't been able to talk, she would have looked completely normal. "Are you a ghost?"

"No, I'm not a ghost," Demerara said. "Come into my flat and I'll tell you the whole story."

"Er—your flat?"

"I don't have much company—forgive the mess."

Demerara walked over to the metal cylinder in the corner, squeezing herself in behind it.

Oz and Lily looked at each other doubtfully and hurried after her. In the wall behind the cylinder was a small door, about a meter high.

"I never noticed that," said Oz.

The door swung open. "You'll have to crawl, but it's not far," said Demerara as she slipped through it.

"I'll go first." Oz dropped down on his hands and knees and crawled after the golden-brown tail.

He found himself in a small space, with such a low ceiling that he could only just sit upright. There was a big metal flashlight hanging from a piece of string, and this lit the clutter of rotting cushions, dog-eared women's magazines and assorted heaps of rubbish, impossible to see in the shadows.

"Move over, I can't get in," Lily said behind him.

"Sorry," said Oz, shifting himself along the bare brick wall so Lily could squeeze in beside him. "What a lovely flat."

"Oh, it's nothing, really!" Demerara purred. "I decorated it myself, with whatever I could find."

"I like the cushions."

"They belonged to Pierre. The big one used to be in my basket."

"Excuse me," said Oz, "but if you're not a ghost, what are you?"

"I'm immortal," Demerara said. "I took part in a certain experiment, and now I can't die."

"Wow—what experiment?"

"It's a long story."

"We shouldn't stay here too long—our parents might notice we're gone."

"Oh, they won't notice a thing," Demerara said breezily. "Let's face it, they never do notice anything—such as the fact that they've just moved into the most magical house in London."

"I knew it!" Lily cried joyfully.

Something near Oz smelled awful. Demerara saw him making a face.

"Oh dear, my food cupboard does smell a bit—Oz, would you pass it over here? It's beside your foot."

Oz's foot was nudging an old cardboard shoe box. He picked it up, and the stink that wafted out of it was terrible.

"Put it behind me," said Demerara. "I'm so sorry, but immortal cats still need to eat, and I don't have any humans to buy me tins of food."

"Poor you," Lily said. "What do you eat?"

"Mice, birds, the bigger insects, anything I can find in people's garbage—that's a beef and chili pizza you can smell. I'm waiting till it's really ripe."

The apparently immortal cat was rolling something metal between her front paws. It was a can of air

freshener without a lid. The twins watched in astonishment as she slammed a paw down on the nozzle and
squirted out a jet of pine-scented Glade; where did cats
buy air freshener?

"How long have you lived in here?" Lily asked.

Demerara's furry golden face creased into a scowl.
"Since 1938, when Pierre was MURDERED!"

"He wasn't murdered," Oz said. "He died in the tram
accident."

"Well, what do you think that was? He knew his life
was in danger. He told me that if he didn't come back, I
must hide here in the safe." Demerara patted something
in the corner. "This room was the safe he built, to keep
his recipes out of enemy hands. These are his books."

In the shadows Oz made out a pile of notebooks
with leather covers. "Are you saying he was a wizard
or something?"

"Pierre was a genius," said Demerara.

"AAARGH!" Lily shrieked suddenly. "A rat!"

"AAAARGH!" screamed a high, whining voice. "Humans!"

In the light of the torch was a skinny rat with a dirty
tail, clutching a small plastic bag.

Oz recognized him at once. "You're the smoking rat!"

"Who—me?"

Demerara let out a furious hiss. "You swore you'd
given it up!"

"But I have given it up, I was only having the one!" The rat dropped the plastic bag, and a heap of revolting cigarette ends fell out. His whiskers quivered at Oz. "Thanks for getting me into trouble."

"Throw them away at once," said Demerara. "I won't have such nasty things in my flat. Lily, you're trembling—what's the matter?"

"I—I don't like rats—"

"My dear, I feel just the same. Believe me, I'd love to kill him."

"But she can't," the rat said, with a whiskery chuckle. "Because I'm as immortal as she is—she's stuck with me."

"Yes, he's quite right," said Demerara. "This is Spike, by the way. I've been trying to civilize him since 1938, and I still haven't succeeded."

"Ha ha, bad luck, old girl!" said Spike. "Oi—where's the food cupboard gone? You've nicked the pigeon bum I was saving!"

"I haven't 'nicked' anything," Demerara said crushingly. "Please try to remember we have guests."

"Is he the Mr. Spike who sent the parcel?" Oz asked.

"No, that was from me; I was just using his name."

"But how on earth did you write the letter?"

The furry golden face was shifty. "Oh, I have certain . . . contacts. There's a witch in the area."

"A witch?" Oz nearly laughed, but did not want to

offend the dignified cat. He didn't want to stop her from talking, either—it was the most entertaining thing he had ever seen.

"I'm not allowed to say anything else," Demerara said grandly. "Let me explain why I summoned you—Spike, kindly don't interrupt."

"Wait till I get myself a snack." The rat scuttled across the heaps of rubbish to the food cupboard and took out an unspeakable something that made Oz and Lily cry, "Yeucch!"

"Spike!" snapped Demerara. "How do you expect them to concentrate with that stink? Put it away and shut up."

"Righto—keep your fur on."

Demerara settled more comfortably on her old cushion. "I might as well start traditionally. Once upon a time, there were three brothers—Isadore, Marcel and Pierre Spoffard. They were triplets, born ten minutes apart. Their father was a French chocolate maker and their mother came from a long line of witches. On their tenth birthday—"

"We have a real witch in the family?" Lily interrupted, her eyes shining.

"Yes, and a very good one. When the boys were ten, their father began to teach them the art of chocolate making and their mother began to teach them magic. They were all very gifted, and most people thought

Isadore was the cleverest of the family, but though Pierre was more modest, he was the real genius."

"You just think that because he worshipped you," Spike said.

Demerara ignored him. "And I don't care what anyone says, it was definitely Pierre who first thought of combining the two—chocolate AND magic! And it was Pierre who came up with their first success, the Wavio bar. This was made of delicious milk chocolate and it curled your hair; Pierre ate a bar of it every morning."

Oz and Lily glanced at each other and had to look away quickly, in case they laughed and stopped Demerara from finishing her story.

"After that," she went on, "they made all kinds of harmless magic chocolate products. For instance, Cherry Growlers made the voice deeper, and were very popular with reedy-voiced politicians. Charm Drops made shy people sparkle at parties, and when the king bought some, Spoffard chocolates became the toast of fashionable London. Oh, those were glorious days! Pierre bought me this sweet little tartan collar and real silver bell."

"Get on with it," said Spike.

Demerara growled crossly. "These children should know about their heritage! The Spoffards reached the giddy height of their success in 1931, when Pierre made a waterproof chocolate boat and rowed it across the Serpentine—with chocolate oars, naturally. Afterward he washed off the pondweed and gave it to an orphanage—your great-great-uncle Pierre was a very kind man. And so was Marcel, your great-great-grandfather. If only Isadore had been more like them!"

"He was a nasty piece of work," said Spike, shaking his greasy head (the human movement looked extremely odd on a rat).

"The trouble started," Demerara said, "when Isadore fell in love. Unfortunately, the young lady didn't like him."

"She said he gave her the creeps," said Spike.

"Shut up, Spike—I'm getting to the important part. Isadore decided to make a very special kind of chocolate that contained a love potion."

"Did it work?" Lily asked.

"Dear me, yes—Isadore's parrot ate some, fell in love with a blackbird in the garden and was never seen again. But the love chocolate didn't work on the young lady because she was already in love with Marcel. She married him, and Isadore never got over it."

"That's what turned him wicked," said Spike.

"He started doing some very dodgy experiments," Demerara said. "That's why this rat and I are immortal—Isadore tested his chocolate on us. So did Pierre, but we didn't mind Pierre's experiments."

"No, his experiments were always kind," Spike agreed. "Like the chocolate that made us talk."

"That must have been a huge success," Lily said. "Everyone would love to talk to their pets."

"Unfortunately," Demerara said, "Pierre was still working on it when he died, and the secret died with him. But the immortality chocolate sprang from Isadore's twisted brain. He knew that rich and powerful people would pay a fortune to stay young forever, and was determined to keep all the money for himself. That's why Isadore survived and the others didn't."

"The tram accident—" Oz said.

"Isadore arranged it all." The cat's strange, yowly voice was full of bitterness. "He murdered Pierre and Marcel and sold the immortality chocolate to the Nazis."

"You mean the German Nazis who started World War Two? Well, that didn't work. The Nazis all died."

"Ha!" squeaked Spike. "That's because Isadore couldn't do the spell on his own!"

"He'd already taken a down payment," Demerara said, "and hidden the money away in a Swiss bank account. But he couldn't deliver the magic chocolate."

"So the Nazis killed him," suggested Lily.

"No, dear," Demerara said. "He pretended to be dead and went into hiding."

"But—but—hang on." Oz was struggling to take this tall story seriously. "Why couldn't he do the spell by himself?"

"Well, Pierre got suspicious, and that's when he made

this safe. He put the recipe books in here and Isadore didn't know a thing about it—that was the advantage he had because he lived above the workshop. And he put his mold in here too. Spike—wipe your paws and get the mold."

"OK." The rat darted across the floor and dived into a pile of musty-smelling rubbish in the darkest corner— squirming about near Oz's sneaker, which felt very unpleasant.

"And try not to breathe on it."

"Ha ha, I won't fart on it either!"

"Must you be so coarse? Oh Lily, what a joy it will be to have some ladylike company!"

Spike dragged something heavy out of the heap and Oz picked it up. It was a small, round metal mold, like a mold for jelly or Play-Doh, in the shape of a blazing sun with a smiling face.

"Thanks, mate," said Spike. "It weighs a ton."

"It's solid gold," Demerara said proudly.

Oz tilted the smiling sun toward the light. Lily crowded close to him to look. The solid gold chocolate mold was a beautiful thing.

"There were three molds," the cat said. "A sun for Pierre, a star for Marcel, and Isadore had the moon. Isadore only had his moon and he needed his brothers' molds to complete the immortality spell. My goodness, he was furious when he couldn't find them!"

"Livid," said Spike. "He was supposed to be dead, but he kept coming back here to look for the stuff—me and the old girl used to watch him and laugh ourselves silly."

Oz yawned. He'd spent the day shifting boxes and he was very tired. "Well, it's been great to meet you both, but I think I'd like to get back to bed now."

"Excuse me," Demerara said, "I haven't finished!"

"Oh—sorry."

"I haven't even told you why I had to bring you here."

"You have a special job for us," Lily said.

"Not me, dear." The cat was solemn. "The government."

Oz was too tired to stop himself from laughing. "What—we're doing a job for the government, like James Bond?"

"I don't see what's so funny," Demerara said stiffly. "As a matter of fact, I work for a secret government department. Three magical humans are needed."

"There's only two of us," Oz pointed out.

"I know!" Demerara hissed. "I can COUNT!"

"She can't," said Spike. "She thought you were triplets, like the Spoffard brothers."

"Shut up, Spike! Didn't I tell you there's a government witch living across the road? That makes three. We'll start tomorrow morning."

"This is daft," Oz said. "Whoever heard of a government witch?"

Demerara gave him a look of withering scorn. "Whoever heard of a talking cat?"

"What are we starting tomorrow?" Lily asked eagerly. "Do you want us to meet you somewhere?"

"I'll come and fetch you, dear." The cat rubbed her soft body against Lily's knee. "And could you leave your tub of disco body glitter open tonight?"

"OK." Lily stroked her. "I'm so glad you're here—thanks for dealing with the wallpaper."

Demerara was nearest the door and wriggled out first. Oz followed, and was very glad to get back into a proper-sized room again—he could hardly breathe in Demerara's smelly "flat." He glanced behind him and blurted out, "Hey—the door's gone!"

They both stared at the blank white wall.

"Wow," said Lily. "No wonder Isadore couldn't find the safe."

"Let's go to bed," Oz said, yawning again. "We're working for the government tomorrow."

4

A Local Witch

"An early start," said the voice of Demerara, "is always best."

To the astonishment of Oz and Lily, the immortal cat strolled into the kitchen the next morning while they were having breakfast with their mother. To their even greater astonishment, her golden-brown fur sparkled with glitter, and the room was filled with a strong smell of chemical perfume.

"Good grief," Mum said, glancing up from her newspaper. "What on earth is that smell? Lily, have you been slathering on that body cream again?"

"She can't hear or see me," said Demerara. "Your parents will be happier if they don't know anything about me." She walked into a shaft of sunlight, glittering all over like a Christmas card, and Oz and Lily both had to struggle not to laugh. "Hurry up—we've a very important meeting, and the local witch is waiting for us outside."

They were both very curious to see this witch.

"Mum, do you need anything from the supermarket?" asked Oz.

"No, thanks."

"Mind if we go out?"

"No—but try not to spend all your money on fizzy drinks."

The twins followed the glittery behind of Demerara outside into Skittle Street. There was no sign of any witch. The only other person in the street was the kid from across the road, still practicing on his skateboard.

"Well?" The cat's mouth was stretched into a smirk. "How do I look?"

"Wonderful!" Lily declared quickly. "Doesn't she, Oz?"

"Er—what?"

She raised her eyebrows meaningfully. "Doesn't Demerara look beautiful this morning?"

"Oh, yes."

"Thank you so much for the body glitter," Demerara said. "The only problem is that it tastes horrid, and I have to keep remembering not to lick myself."

Oz snorted with laughter, but Lily nudged him crossly.

"It so suits you," she told the cat.

"I wanted to make an effort; I'm not allowed to be invisible in the office and I like to look smart. Lily, dear—

could you paint my claws later with some of your lovely nail polish? I promise not to scratch you."

"I'd be happy to," said Lily.

"I can't decide between the gold and the bright pink."

"Excuse me—" Oz didn't want to spend the whole morning talking about makeup, and he didn't want the boy across the road to think they were crazy for talking to a cat. He lowered his voice. "What office? And where's this witch?"

"Over there." Demerara nodded calmly toward the skateboarding boy.

"Him?" Oz had been waiting for an excuse to talk to this boy, but he didn't look the slightest bit witchlike—weren't witches always old ladies? "He can't be a witch!"

Demerara strolled calmly across the road. She jumped gracefully onto the low wall beside the path and stared at the boy as he whisked past on his skateboard.

"Good morning, Caydon," she said.

The boy—Caydon—looked thunderstruck and immediately fell off.

Oz and Lily ran over to the boy now lying in the path, gaping at Demerara.

"Are you OK?" Oz asked.

"I don't know," Caydon said faintly. "Is that—your cat?"

"Yes," said Lily.

Painfully he stood up and dusted himself off. "I must be hearing things—I swear it spoke to me—its mouth moved and everything—"

"Of course I spoke!" Demerara snapped impatiently. "You're the witch I requested."

"What? What's going on?" Caydon looked at Oz and Lily. "This is a trick, right?"

"There's no trick," Oz said. "It's—well, you see—"

"It's magic," said Lily. "And apparently you're involved."

"Me? I don't know anything about magic!"

"Haven't you had your orders?" Demerara asked. "Oh bother, I was hoping they'd send someone more experienced."

"This is too weird," Caydon said. "I think I must be dreaming—or maybe I'm ill—"

Oz was starting to worry that they'd got the wrong person, until Demerara said, "If you weren't dripping with magic, young man, you wouldn't be able to hear me."

Caydon was bewildered. "Of course I can hear you—someone please tell me what's going on!"

"Look, sorry about this," said Oz. "I didn't believe it either, not at first. But she really does talk."

"You're Oz, right? I heard your dad calling you when you moved in."

"Yes, and this is my sister, Lily. We're twins."

"Cool," said Caydon. "Wish I had a twin. I live with my mum and my gran—that's our flat, with the purple door. Which one of your parents plays the violin?"

Oz wasn't sure he wanted to admit to this, but before he could say anything, Lily jumped in with "That's Oz."

Caydon was impressed. "You're seriously good."

"He's a genius," said Lily.

"Shuddup." Oz was embarrassed.

It didn't seem to put Caydon off. "How old are you two?"

"Eleven," Oz said.

"Me too. What school are you going to in September?"

"Sir Richard Whittington."

"Great," said Caydon, "that's where I'm going too. A lot of places round here are named after him—my gran works at the Whittington Hospital." He turned to Lily. "Are you a genius too?"

"No," she said stiffly. "Oz got all the talent. I'm rubbish at everything, because I'm dyslexic."

"A boy in my class had that," Caydon said. "He set fire to a shed in the playground."

Lily scowled at him. "You might think I'm weird, but I don't go round setting fire to things, thank you very much. The boy in your class was probably angry because he was sick of not understanding, and not being able to make things stick in his head."

Her voice was fierce, and for a moment Caydon was startled. "I don't think you're weird." He smiled suddenly. "But your cat is the weirdest thing I've ever seen."

"Her name's Demerara," said Lily.

Caydon was starting to get over his shock. "Why's she covered with glitter?"

"It's to make me look elegant," Demerara said. "Now, let's stop this chitchat and get to our appointment."

"Where's this appointment, then?"

"It's in the MI6 building beside the river," said Demerara.

Caydon burst out laughing. "Yeah, right—so you're a secret agent."

"Yes, but I can't talk about my work here." The cat's bright green eyes glinted crossly at the "witch" from across the road. "We'll go on the bus."

"Hang on," said Oz. "We don't know the right buses to get to MI6."

"Caydon does."

The twins looked at Caydon.

"Matter of fact," he said, "I do know a lot about buses. It's a hobby of mine. My mum's a driver on the 390."

"Are cats allowed on buses?" Lily asked.

"I'll be riding in a pet carrier," said Demerara. "Caydon, go and get it and we'll be off."

Caydon was surprised. "We do have a pet carrier—our cat died last year, but we haven't chucked it out yet—wait there."

"You believe in magic now," said Lily.

"Since I'm talking to a cat," Caydon said cheerfully, "I don't have much choice, do I? And I don't have anything else to do today." He picked up his skateboard and ran into the flat on the ground floor with a purple front door. A moment later, he emerged with a large plastic pet carrier.

"Open the little door, please," Demerara said.

Caydon opened the end of the pet carrier and the fussy cat trotted inside.

Lily bent down to look at her through the bars. "Are you comfy in there, Demerara?"

"Yes—if nobody swings me about too much. Now, let's get moving."

"Well," said Caydon, "I didn't expect to spend my day taking orders from a cat."

Oz thought it was nice of him to be so calm about it. "Sorry you had to get involved."

"Sorry?" Caydon grinned. "Are you joking? This is the most fun I've had in ages!"

Even if Demerara had got the wrong witch, Caydon was extremely useful. He knew exactly the right buses they should take down to the huge, modern MI6 building beside the Thames, which Oz had only ever seen in one of the Bond films.

"I know the one," Caydon said. "He smashes through the wall in a speedboat."

It turned out that Oz and Caydon had a lot in common. They sat together on the bus, talking about computer games, the basketball hoop that Oz's dad was going to put up in the yard when the weeds were cleared, and the enormous toy car track they could build on Oz's bedroom floor if Caydon brought his track from across the road. In between, Oz filled Caydon in on the story of the Spoffards and the magic chocolate.

Lily sat behind them with Demerara. Caydon wasn't taking any notice of Lily; whenever she spoke he looked at Oz, as if she didn't exist. She would have felt left out if she hadn't had the cat to talk to.

"But you mustn't say anything—it'll freak out the other passengers to hear a cat talking."

"Oh, all right," Demerara sighed, from the depths of the pet carrier. "But it's so hard—I haven't had a refined conversation since 1938."

They were on the top deck and it was nearly empty. Lily looked round carefully before she asked, "Can't you have one with Spike?"

"No," said Demerara. "I try to make allowances—I know Spike hasn't had my advantages in life—but a rat from the sewers is no companion for a posh animal like me."

Lily didn't like rats, but she felt sorry for Spike; it couldn't be much fun spending all those years with a cat who despised you. "How did he get to be immortal, anyway?"

"By mistake—it started when Pierre left some of the talking-chocolate out overnight." The voice floating out of the pet carrier was scornful. "Next morning, we woke up to the horrible sound of a rat's drunken singing. For some reason, Pierre thought it was FUNNY"— she spat this word out—"and he decided to keep Spike for experimental purposes. Rats never mind being experimented on. Unfortunately, when Pierre died, I was stuck with him."

"We're here," said Caydon.

They were in the middle of the city, beside the wide, gray-green river. The MI6 building was huge and modern, made of slabs of pinkish stone. Lily, Oz and Caydon stared at it. The gleaming entrance hall was full of smartly dressed people with plastic IDs hanging around their necks, all looking very busy and important. Two policemen stood outside the main entrance.

Oz, who was carrying Demerara, bent down toward her and asked "What do we do next?"

"Obviously, we go inside!" Demerara hissed impatiently.

"I don't think three kids with a pet carrier are going to get very far."

"Just show them my card."

"What card?"

"I have it with me inside the carrier."

Lily opened the door—and there was a small, plastic-covered card sitting under one of the cat's front paws. "Where did this come from?"

"Never mind where it came from. It's my secret ID."

They all looked at Demerara's ID, which was nothing but a bar code and a paw mark.

Caydon said, "I've a feeling this is going to be embarrassing."

5

A Job for the Department

The policeman outside was nice, but obviously thought they were messing about. He took Demerara's card and chuckled.

"Where did you get this? It's a pretty good imitation of one of our passes—except for the paw mark."

"Kindly swipe it at once and let us in!" an angry voice mewed from inside the pet carrier.

The young policeman raised his eyebrows, automatically thinking Lily must have said it.

Turning red as a brick, she said, "Er—please."

"Oh, all right, if it will make you go away." The policeman swiped Demerara's card and his face immediately changed. "Oh—it says here—I'd better take you to the sergeant."

The three kids made faces of surprise at each other. The young policeman was actually leading them into the MI6 building. They followed him across a long polished floor to a desk, where they were handed over to another, older policeman.

He looked at the card, and at them. "Oh, yes, this lot are on the priority list. Come on."

It was like some mad dream. Oz asked, "Are you—are you sure we're the right people?"

"Course I am—not many people bring their pets in here."

"Pets!" hissed Demerara. "How DARE he? Do I look like someone's PET?"

"Sorry, ma'am." The second policeman was amazingly unsurprised by a talking cat. He took them to an elevator, and then to an office, where there was a man in a gray suit drinking coffee.

"Something for your department, sir," the policemen said.

"Yes," the man in the suit said calmly, "the desk called me. Thank you, Sergeant; I'll take it from here."

Oz and Lily caught sight of each other's stunned faces: why did everyone seem to be expecting them? It seemed that the show-off cat had been telling the truth; she really was working for the government.

The man in the suit said, "This way, please."

He took them to another lift, which he worked with a key. It whisked them right up to the top floor. The man in the suit knocked on a door opposite the lift.

A woman's voice said, "Come in."

Oz was nearest the door, so he opened it, and the three of them walked into another very white and tidy office, with walls of filing cabinets and a large computer.

The woman was about Emily Spoffard's age, wearing a smart navy suit. She looked up from her desk, smiling. "Hello, Demerara."

"Hello," said Demerara. "Let me out, someone."

Oz put down the pet carrier (which was a relief; the cat was no lightweight, and the smell of the body glitter was making him dizzy) and Demerara trotted out onto the carpet.

"Lovely glitter," the woman said kindly.

"Thank you, B62. As you can see, I've brought the children."

B62 looked at them. "You said they were triplets."

"The rat who works for me made a mistake—but I managed to draft in this witch, Caydon Campbell."

B62 pressed a few keys on her computer. "Oh yes, that's all in order."

"I'm not a witch," Caydon said.

"Of course you are. You're in the system."

"That's the first I've heard of it!"

Demerara absently licked her paw, then spat crossly. "Ugh—I forgot! Is J ready for us?"

"Go right in." B62 stood up to open a polished wooden door. "They're here, sir."

Oz, Lily and Caydon walked into a grand office dominated by a big antique desk. The whole thing was so peculiar, they had to keep glancing at each other to remind themselves this was not a dream.

A tall man with gray hair stood in the window with his back to them, reading a file.

"Well, Demerara—you've put us through a lot of trouble. You'd better be right about this emergency."

"Of course I'm right!" The glittery cat was indignant. "Here are my three helpers."

He turned round to face them. "Hello. My name is J. Please sit down."

There were three chairs in front of the desk. Oz, Lily and Caydon sat down while Demerara made a graceful leap onto the desk.

J pressed a buzzer. A moment later B62 came in holding a pile of papers. Caydon nudged Oz's foot with his and mouthed, "Moneypenny!"

"I'm glad you know about James Bond," J said. "It might make this whole business a little easier for you to understand. The first thing I must ask you to do is sign the Official Secrets Act."

Oz, Lily and Caydon exchanged looks of bafflement—was the man joking?

B62 laid three sheets of paper and three pens on the desk in front of them.

"I signed it ages ago," Demerara said proudly.

"Nothing to worry about," B62 said. "You're just promising never to tell anyone about this place."

"I won't say a word," Lily said. "Nobody would believe me, anyway. I bet this is the part of the government that deals with magic."

J chuckled. "Not quite—but close enough. Officially my department doesn't exist. Officially I'm not here and this room is a broom closet. I can't tell you more until you've signed." He leaned across the desk toward them. "We're trusting you with some highly sensitive information."

Suddenly, this was all looking serious. Oz, Lily and Caydon signed the pieces of paper.

"Caydon R. Campbell," Caydon said. "The R stands for—"

"Robert," J finished for him. "Yes, we know."

"What—you know about me?"

"Oh, yes," said B62. "You support Arsenal, hate spinach and play the saxophone."

"Wha—but—" Caydon was flabbergasted. "MI6 have been spying on me?"

"We're not MI6," J said. "This is the SMU—the Secret Ministry of the Unexplained. We deal with anything—er—unexplained that might be a threat to national security. You're probably wondering why the SMU needs the help of three eleven-year-olds. I must admit, I wondered myself."

"But I insisted!" Demerara spat. "We MUST have the children, or the spells won't work—and we won't have a HOPE of retrieving the mold."

J sighed and shook his head. "It wasn't easy; I had to get clearance from the prime minister."

"Wow," Oz said. "The prime minister knows about us."

"Not officially, of course," J said. "Now, pay attention. We have reason to believe that Isadore Spoffard is trying to sell his immortality chocolate again. Last time it was to the Nazis. This time we think he's working for a group of terrorists known as the Schmertz Gang. We have reason to believe these very dangerous people are planning a major attack, probably in London. Their leaders want to rule the world, which they think will be possible if they live forever. That's why they need Isadore's chocolate."

The sound of Isadore's name chilled Oz's spine, and he knew Lily had the same feeling. "He's still alive?"

"Very much so; the SMU has been keeping tabs on him since 1938." J tapped a key on his keyboard and the painting of the queen on the wall behind him changed to a photograph of a dark-haired man with a narrow black mustache and a thin, sour face. "Isadore Spoffard, just before he killed his brothers." He clicked rapidly through a series of photographs of the same sour face with different hairstyles. "He's a master of disguise. Over the years he's used all sorts of names—Tom Dribway, Quentin Cobbler, Heinz Schmidt, Professor Pillick and Mrs. Harriet Wong."

"We haven't seen him in Skittle Street yet," Demerara said, "but it's only a matter of time. He wants the recipe for immortality."

"And I'm sure I don't need to tell you," J said, "how dreadful it would be if such a thing fell into the hands of wicked people no bomb or bullet could stop."

This was scary—and incredibly exciting. Their wicked great-great-uncle was still alive.

"What do we have to do?" Oz asked.

J and B62 looked at each other. "I don't like it," J said. "But there's no other way. The immortality chocolate can't be made without all three of the golden molds. Isadore still has his moon, of course. Pierre's sun is safely sealed in Demerara's flat. But Marcel's star isn't nearly so well protected. We need to find it and get it to a much safer place—in a special government vault—because it's better to keep the molds in different places. We need your magical powers to find it."

"I never knew we had magical powers; does it mean we can do spells?" Lily asked.

"Yes, in theory," J said. "But you don't need to do anything complicated now; you just have to be there." He broke off to sigh, "I must be honest; this could be dangerous, and it was quite a problem getting clearance."

"There's no other way." Demerara was firm. "The immortality chocolate can't be made without all three of them—and Marcel's mold has been lost since 1938. My personal opinion is that he had it with him when he died in the accident."

"That means it must be at the bottom of the river," Oz said. "Why do you need us to find it? Couldn't you just send down some divers?"

"We've tried all the ordinary methods."

"But—hang on—" Oz was trying to get the complicated story straight. "All three brothers were on the tram—right? So why didn't Isadore just grab the mold from Marcel while he was drowning?"

"That's a very good question," J said. "And the truth is, we don't quite know. It's possible that the mold had some sort of inbuilt resistance to wickedness. We do know that Isadore has searched the riverbed at least twenty times since 1938, but he never found a thing. This department—which, of course, doesn't exist—has been assigned a special unit of river police. They will contact you."

"What should we tell our parents? Are they included in the Official Secrets Act?" Oz asked.

"Ah." J was a little uncomfortable. "Thank you for reminding me; it's rather important. I'm sorry, but your parents must know absolutely nothing about this. We'll provide you with excellent cover stories."

"I don't think I'm that good at lying," Caydon said. "My gran can see through walls."

"That won't be a problem. We've taken certain steps to stop your parents from noticing anything. They won't be asking any awkward questions."

"Are you sure?" Caydon was doubtful.

J and B62 exchanged smiles. "Not even your gran, I guarantee it." He stood up. "Thank you all very much— and jolly good luck."

He shook hands with them, and shook Demerara's paw. A few minutes later the three children and their pet carrier were being escorted out of the building.

"Incredible," said Oz. "We're secret agents! What do we do now?"

Caydon glanced at his watch. "This secret agent had better get home—before his gran finds out he hasn't picked up the dry cleaning."

6

Secret Agents

The government agency that did not exist was very efficient. Next morning, Dad said, "Why didn't you two tell me you'd signed up for this diving course?"

"Diving? What're you talking about?" Lily began.

Oz nudged her. "We—we forgot."

Dad was reading an official-looking letter. "Well, it's a very good course, run by the river police. They're sending someone to pick you both up this afternoon."

"It sounds a bit dangerous," said Mum.

"I think it's great," Dad said firmly. "What with moving houses and the new baby coming, Oz and Lily aren't having much of a summer holiday this year—they deserve a bit of fun."

"But Lily," Mum said, "you won't like diving; you don't even like swimming."

Lily tried to look casual, though her stomach was going up and down like a lift. "I've changed my mind."

"Well, if you're sure—Bruce, do they need any special clothes?"

"Just ordinary luggage for one night away," Dad said, looking at the letter. "Everything else is provided."

"I'm terrified," Lily admitted to Demerara, when the two of them were alone in her bedroom. "I hate the thought of being deep underwater. But I knew it was our first job, so I tried not to show it."

The immortal cat was lying on the bed with one paw placed on a cushion, while Lily painted her claws with gold nail polish. "You mustn't worry," she purred. "The SMU takes good care of its agents—it'll cost millions if you die."

"I suppose that's a comfort," said Lily. "Are you coming?"

"Of course, dear—I'm your commanding officer."

"If you're there I'll have someone to talk to. Oz hasn't said one word to me since he met Caydon. I might as well be invisible."

"Boys need other boys," Demerara said. "It's the same with cats. In the meantime, you and I can be girls together. And you'll make new human friends when you go to your new school."

"No, I won't. It'll be just like our last school. The girls there thought I was mad and laughed at me because I can't learn long division."

"What's long division?"

Lily groaned softly. "I don't know! My teachers keep me in at recess to explain it—and then I think I've got it—and then I forget it again the next day! And everybody else just seems to know without being told—even people who seem a lot thicker than me."

"Is it a sort of spell?"

"No," said Lily. "If it was, I could see the point. It's math."

"Well, I know you'll make friends. I've been watching the children walking to school since 1927, and some things never change."

"I hope you're right."

"I'm always right, dear." The cat broke off suddenly, and her green eyes darted suspiciously around the walls. "Do you hear something? Are these roses behaving themselves?"

"Yes." Lily glanced at the wallpaper; the faces of the yellow roses were beaming, and there was somehow an atmosphere of cheekiness.

"Hmm. Anyway, as I was saying, I'm sure lots of fascinating friends are waiting in your future—and you'll also see the point of Caydon."

"Why do we need him?"

"We just do." The cat's eyes were flinty; Lily was starting to recognize her stubborn look. "All the spells need three witches—one for each mold. Now please dry my claws with your hair dryer."

"OK." Lily stood up to fetch her hair dryer, and this time she thought she heard scattered tittering from the wallpaper roses.

"Shut up!" squeaked Demerara. "Any more bother from you lot and I'll have you painted over! Lily, when my claws are dry, the fur round my neck needs more volume—do you have any curlers?"

Lily was almost glad when her mother called upstairs that the diving man had arrived. Dangerous diving couldn't be more stressful than being Demerara's beautician; the cat was a little furry slave driver.

There was a young policeman in the kitchen, with very short blond hair and large pink ears. His feet, in their thick police boots, were enormous. When he stood up to shake hands with Lily, the whole room seemed to shrink.

"This is Alan," Mum said happily. "He works for the river police—isn't it wonderful that they're teaching London schoolkids to dive?" Incredibly, she seemed to think this was the most normal thing in the world.

She turned away from them, and Alan quickly showed Oz and Lily a plastic card like Demerara's, with a fingerprint instead of a paw mark.

"We'd better be off," he said. "Thanks for the tea, Mrs. Spoffard."

"Goodbye, darlings, I hope you have a lovely time." Mum hugged Oz and Lily.

Lily had to make an effort not to cling to her; Mum mustn't know how scared she was. "See you tomorrow."

Caydon was waiting in the street, sitting on the low wall in front of the flats with his backpack at his feet. Demerara sat on the wall beside him.

"Hi, Caydon," Alan said, shaking his hand. "I hope you didn't have any trouble getting away."

"No, Gran was all for it," Caydon said. "She says it'll be good for me to do as I'm told for a change."

"Quite right," said Demerara. "When you're diving, obeying orders is a matter of life and death."

The young policeman was grinning all over his pink face. "So you're the talking cat—I thought my sergeant was having a laugh!"

"Did you indeed," Demerara said crossly. "How very unprofessional."

Alan glanced at his watch. "Where's the talking rat?"

"I didn't know Spike was coming," Lily said.

"Unfortunately, we can't do without his underworld connections," Demerara said.

"She means other rats," said Alan. "This Spike is a legendary figure among his own kind."

Demerara examined one of her painted claws. "I know where he'll be—go round the corner and look for the drain with smoke coming out of it."

At that moment a small brown shape scuttled across

the empty street toward them. Spike was dirtier than ever, and very out of breath. "Ugh! Ugh! Am I late?"

"Hi," said Alan.

"You're the river policeman, are you? Nice to meet you, and you don't need to worry about security—I've got a special squad waiting inside a broken pipe under Westminster Bridge."

Alan had a black car with darkened windows. He put Oz and Caydon in the backseat, with Demerara sitting between them. Lily took the front seat. Spike was banished to the trunk, because Demerara said he smelled disgustingly of smoke and she refused to travel anywhere near him.

Once again, Lily found herself feeling sorry for the sewer rat. He was rather disgusting, but he was also very easygoing; he didn't at all mind riding in the trunk.

Oz asked, "Can you say where you're taking us?"

"You don't need to know where," said Alan, "but I can tell you that you'll be taking a practice dive in our testing tank—have any of you done scuba diving before?"

"I've been snorkeling," Oz said. "That was pretty good."

"We're going scuba diving?" Lily's voice trembled. "I can't do that—I don't even know what it is!"

"It stands for self-contained underwater breathing

apparatus," said Caydon. "You wear an oxygen tank, and you can get down really deep—like those guys in TV fish shows."

"The Thames isn't that deep," Oz said. "It would be really cool if we were diving in the sea."

Alan gave Lily an encouraging smile. "The first dive is the worst—I was scared stiff."

"Really?"

"I thought I wouldn't be able to breathe down there."

This was one of Lily's fears, and it was a relief to hear Alan mention it so casually. "Is it very hard?"

"The secret is to forget about it and breathe normally."

She shivered. "Suppose something goes wrong?"

"That's why I'm here," said Alan. "To make sure nothing does."

"I always sing myself a little song." Demerara's voice floated at them from the back seat.

"Yes, but you're immortal and you don't need breathing equipment," Alan said.

Lily found that she felt less paralyzed with nerves; Alan was very confident. "How did you get involved in the SMU?"

"I shouldn't really tell you, but since you've signed the Official Secrets Act—I was just a normal constable in the river police, until I found a mermaid."

He had all their attention now.

"Seriously?" Caydon asked.

"Oh, yes. It was about three in the morning, and a member of the public called to say they'd heard someone screaming under one of the bridges. We took the boat to have a look—and there she was."

"What was she like?" Lily asked.

"She was no beauty, that's for sure," Alan said. "Her top half was like a little old woman, all covered with seaweed and screaming her head off. Her bottom half was the back end of a fish, and she'd got her tail caught on an old shopping cart someone had chucked in. The guy who was with me fainted, but I kept my head and cut her loose."

"What happened to her?"

"I don't know—she just slipped away into the water and she was gone. The SMU recruited me the next day. You wouldn't believe all the unexplained stuff in that river!"

"Are there many mermaids?"

Alan said, "No, I was lucky—you only get a sighting every hundred years or so, when the weather's very bad and they get washed in from the sea. But I've seen giant octopuses, I've towed away a dead sea dragon, I've threatened the captain of a ghost ship with arrest—it's the most interesting job I've ever had."

"How could you arrest a ghost?" Oz asked.

"Ghost ships have to abide by regulations, same as

everyone else," said Alan. "And I was working with a ghost policeman. You meet all sorts in this line of work."

He was driving south, toward the river, and stopped suddenly at a large, dull building like a school, tucked away in a dull side street.

"Head office," Alan said. "It doesn't exist officially, of course. Come on."

They all got out of the car. Alan opened the trunk and found Spike fast asleep on Lily's backpack. His unsavory little body left a smear of dirt, which Lily tried not to mind about; he got enough telling-off from Demerara.

Alan led the three children and two talking animals into the SMU's officially nonexistent building.

"First things first," Alan said cheerfully. "You'll be issued ID cards, and someone will take your measurements."

Caydon pointed at Spike. "Do they have special tiny equipment for him?"

"I don't need it." Spike laughed wheezily. "A bit of drowning never did me any harm."

"Stop showing off," Demerara said. "You should be down in the sewers—you don't want to keep your fans waiting."

"OK, old girl." The good-tempered rat waved a paw and trotted out into the street. "See you later!" he said, slipping down the nearest drain.

The policeman at reception handed Alan a cardboard box. "The cat needs to sign for this—it's the stuff she requested from the secret vault."

"Oh, yes." Demerara made one of her leaps up to the desk. "I hope it hasn't gone bad."

Lily, despite her nerves, was interested to watch the cat "signing" a thick book by putting her paw on an ink pad and making a print in a thick ledger. The strangest thing about this place was its lack of strangeness—it was like a very ordinary office, and none of the staff were at all surprised to meet animals who talked.

Alan took the cardboard box. He opened the lid to reveal three glossy chocolate coins. "These are safe, right?"

"It's one of Pierre's recipes," Demerara said proudly. "I moved his leftover magic chocolate into the ministry's high-security preservation vault—to be honest, I didn't trust Spike not to eat it. These are Duck Drops, which improve people's swimming."

Lily was relieved to hear they would be getting some magical help; these sounded like just the thing for someone like her, who couldn't even swim a whole length at Washford Waterworld.

"Well—" Alan looked at the chocolate coins and smiled. "I'm jealous—they smell great."

They did have a lovely rich, sweet scent, and were made of the very best creamy, glossy chocolate—you'd never think it had been languishing in a vault for years. Oz and Caydon ate theirs quickly, but Lily let her chocolate coin dissolve slowly on her tongue; the taste was wonderful.

And she did feel a bit less scared of being underwater.

7

The Tram in the River

"OK, let's run through it one more time," Alan said. "You three stick close to me on the way down, and when we get to the tram, watch for Ms. Demerara's signal to join hands—just like we practiced."

It was just past two o'clock in the morning, as they could see from the face of Big Ben looming above them. Oz, Caydon, Lily and Alan stood on the deck of a small motorboat. They were all wearing wet suits, oxygen tanks, large goggles, nose clips and mouthpieces.

No amount of Duck Drops could stop Lily from being nervous. The test dive that afternoon had been in a plain tank like a very deep swimming pool. The water that lapped and sucked around the launch looked as black as ink, and filthy; jumping into the Thames was going to be much more dangerous. Oz and Caydon were hugely excited, but they had gone very quiet. Alan had fixed powerful flashlights to their goggles, and they were all joined to the boat by long ropes. Alan took Lily's hand and the two of them did the backward roll into the water, just as they had practiced.

Slipping into the cold, dark underwater world was a shock, and Lily had to make herself concentrate on keeping her breathing steady—no matter what Alan said about breathing "normally," she couldn't feel normal with the mouthpiece and nose clip. Very cautiously she dared to make a few movements with her arms and legs, and was surprised by how fast she could propel herself with her flippers.

Demerara suddenly swam into the beam of the flashlight, looking so funny that Lily nearly upset her breathing by laughing. The cat had little flippers on her back paws, and wore a tiny red wetsuit with "Property of Her Majesty's Government" stamped on the side. She did not need oxygen, but the water made her sneeze out clouds of bubbles.

Alan was holding another flashlight, and he pointed it down into the deepest depths of the river. The beam caught at strange growths and spars and twists of barnacled rubbish in the gloom, and Lily tried not to think of the weird things Alan had come across in his job with the River Police Unit of the SMU—she didn't fancy meeting a sea dragon, dead or alive. She was certain, however, that the magic chocolate was working; it didn't stop her from being scared, but it did make her amazingly confident and graceful in the water. She even dared to let go of Alan's hand.

In front of her, Demerara suddenly got agitated. She darted and swooped like a demented four-legged acrobat, and her mouth moved in a storm of bubbles.

They had found the tram.

"There won't be any dead bodies, will there?" Lily had asked Alan that afternoon.

"Of course not."

"And—no ghosts?"

"It was thoroughly checked by the ghost patrol," Alan had assured her. "You don't need to worry about anything except finding that golden mold."

It was comforting to know that this terrible place—where twenty-four people, including Oz and Lily's great-great-grandfather and great-great uncle, had perished in 1938—was not haunted. All the same, in the beams of the flashlight, the wrecked tram did make Lily catch her breath. It had sunk down into the mud, until only the tops of the windows (and half a ghostly advertisement for Bovril) were visible.

Demerara seemed to know exactly what she was doing, and slipped inside one of the windows, where the glass had shattered. It was a narrow opening. Alan had a kind of pickax attached to his belt, and he used this to make it bigger.

The three children had their instructions. Caydon

swam after the cat, Oz followed Caydon, Lily went next, and Alan swam in last.

Lily paused to concentrate on her breathing; so far, everything was going well. They were inside the wrecked tram. She felt herself sinking slowly into the soft, oozy mud until it came up to her waist. The beams of light shone through the murky Thames water, showing the very tops of wooden seats and shadowy advertisements for Sunlight Soap and Stephens's Ink. The twins and Caydon joined hands.

"You'll know the sign when you get it," Demerara had told them.

They had practiced the joining of hands in the testing tank, and there had been no hint of a magical sign—but something was different now. For the first time in ages, the other voice the twins had sensed when they were small was among them. Lily's heart was beating hard, yet she wasn't afraid. It was like being part of a machine; she could almost feel the electricity fizzing through them. She felt like they were being tugged toward something—the three of them, clutching one another's hands, squelched and sucked along the narrow passage between the sunken seats.

A bolt of searing heat shot through their arms, flinging them all apart—for a few seconds Lily lost her footing and had to scramble frantically not to disappear into the mud.

This was the sign Demerara had been waiting for; she plopped into the mud, sending out a great fountain of dirt. The water cleared and there was the triumphant cat, wearing something gold on her head; years at the bottom of the Thames had not dimmed the magic metal of the lost mold.

They had found it—or it had found them. Oz, Caydon and Lily did underwater high fives. Demerara turned somersaults of triumph. Alan tucked the precious object carefully into a special pocket on his wetsuit and made the thumbs-up sign—mission accomplished.

What happened next caught them all completely off guard. Alan saw them safely out of the tram. At the very moment he came out himself, something—someone—rushed at him through the dirty water like a torpedo.

It took Lily a second to make sense of what she was seeing.

A thin man in a white suit, wearing no diving equipment whatsoever, was wrestling violently with Alan. He bashed the head of the river policeman against the side of the tram, snatched the golden mold out of his pocket, and paused to laugh a horrible, silent, underwater laugh, his face veiled by a blizzard of bubbles.

Isadore.

The evil immortal chocolatier didn't have enough

magic to find the mold by himself; he had been waiting until they found it for him.

Alan was slumped in the water—had Isadore killed him? Caydon swooped forward and bravely kicked the mold from Isadore's hand. It dropped down into the ooze on the riverbed. To Lily's horror, Isadore—silently screaming with fury—gave Caydon a tremendous swipe that sent him rocketing away toward the surface.

The golden chocolate mold gleamed in the mud, but Oz and Lily had to help Alan, and quickly swam to his side.

And then everything was a maelstrom of underwater madness.

Through her goggles Lily saw Isadore—bizarre in his white suit, with brown-and-white lace-ups on his feet instead of flippers—dive for the mold with outstretched hands.

The very second before his hand closed round it, the golden mold was whisked away by a stout cat in a wetsuit, who was immediately surrounded by a flock of small dark shapes—hundreds of swimming rats, carrying her away to the surface.

The look of fury on Isadore's face was horrible to see. His mouth opened in a silent scream, and he lunged at Oz, grabbing his arm and tugging him away into the murky depths of the river.

"I know this is easy to say," Alan murmured, "but try not to worry too much. We'll have agents searching round the clock—and he won't be harmed while we have two of the molds."

Lily had finally stopped sobbing. She was calm and exhausted, sick with misery. "And are you sure our parents won't notice Oz has been kidnapped?"

"Quite sure," Alan said. "The department's very good at cover stories."

"But Isadore murdered his own brothers—what'll he do to Oz?"

"I still think we should get back in the river and look for him," Caydon said.

"He'll have gone by now," said Alan.

"Gone where?"

"Nobody knows where Isadore's hideout is, I'm afraid—but I know they'll put their best people on it."

"Let me tell you what I'd like to do to that Isadore Spoffard," Spike said furiously. "I'd like to watch a whole army of rats tearing him limb from limb."

"Never mind," Alan said. "You and your army got the mold—it's been taken straight to the SMU vault."

"Do you really have your own army?" Caydon asked.

"Just a few mates who owe me favors," said Spike.

Big Ben loudly struck three above their heads. They

were sitting in a cozy riverside police hut, and had changed out of their diving gear into ordinary clothes that now felt deliciously comfortable. Alan was fine—he had only been stunned—and he had kindly bought them all cups of tea and egg sandwiches from a twenty-four-hour stall on the Embankment.

They had been joined by Alan's boss, a plump, bald sergeant who looked far too ordinary to be dealing with the unexplained. They were all—even the angry animals—talking quietly, because the sergeant was on the phone to the prime minister.

"Thank you, sir." He switched off his phone. "He's deeply concerned, and he's making young Oz his number one priority. He wants hourly reports."

Lily felt a little more hopeful; the prime minister was the most important person in the country, and that had to mean they would find her brother quickly.

"I hope he didn't mind being disturbed in the middle of the night," Demerara said.

"No, he said it was fine—he's taking this business very seriously. And he was up anyway with the baby."

Alan had not forgotten the animals when he was buying their early breakfast: Demerara lapped at a bowl of milk, and Spike chomped disgustingly through a bacon roll.

"Boy, this is lovely! Fancy a bite, old girl?"

"No, thank you," Demerara said primly. "I'm watching my waistline."

"Well, you are quite pudgy," Caydon said.

"PUDGY?" The cat was highly offended. "Lily, tell me honestly—am I pudgy?"

"I like to see the old girl with a bit of meat on her," Spike said. "That's what a fine figure looked like in my day."

"Crudely put," Demerara said, "but he means it kindly. And I must admit he's been useful. Wait till we get hold of Isadore! He might be immortal, but we can still make him SUFFER!"

"You're a hard cat, Demerara," Alan said. "I wouldn't like to get on your wrong side."

"We're paying Isadore back for what he did to us," Spike said, sucking on a piece of bacon. "When he was experimenting with his immortality recipe, he left me burning in a fire all night to see if I'd die. I came out like a charred sausage—my hair didn't grow back for weeks."

"And he left me trapped in a bucket of water for a whole weekend," said Demerara.

Lily's swollen eyes smarted; if she'd had any tears left, she would have cried again. This great-great-uncle of hers was incredibly wicked and it was agony to think of Oz in his clutches.

Caydon yawned loudly. "I am SO tired! And when

I got up this morning—yesterday morning—I didn't even know I was going scuba diving. Can we go home yet?"

"As soon as it's a decent time to wake your parents," the sergeant said. "You've both done a terrific job tonight."

"No, we haven't," said Lily. "We've lost Oz—it's been a disaster."

"My dear Lily." Demerara put a paw on Lily's arm. "Alan's quite right—Isadore won't lay a finger on Oz."

"He won't give him back unless he gets something in exchange—I don't care what it is, you have to give it to him! Let him have the stupid molds!"

"Sorry," the sergeant said gently. "That's the one thing we can't do. You have to be very brave and trust us to do this our way. Isadore is dangerous enough with only one mold."

Lily was too tired to argue anymore. Despite the dreadfulness of everything, she fell asleep the moment she got into the car, and didn't wake up until they were on Skittle Street and Caydon was shaking her shoulder. She stumbled out onto the pavement. "Alan, wait— what shall I say to Mum and Dad?"

"It's been dealt with," Alan said. "All you have to do is try not to look worried."

"That's going to be impossible."

"Hope Oz comes back soon," Caydon said. "It'll be so boring without him."

"Thanks a lot," Lily snapped.

"Well, sorry, but you know what I mean—you don't like the stuff we like doing."

"You two are supposed to be working together," Demerara said, stretching. "It's no good squabbling—if you want to help Oz, you must put your differences aside. Alan, don't forget Spike."

Alan opened the trunk and a cloud of smoke puffed out.

"SPIKE!" shrieked Demerara. "How DARE you smoke in a government vehicle?"

"Ugh! Ugh! I've been under stress!"

"I'll give you STRESS, you unspeakable rodent!"

The young river policeman picked up the grimy rat and dropped him on the pavement.

"I'm getting out of here—see you, kids!" said Spike, dashing into the gutter and jumping down the nearest drain before Demerara could pounce on him.

"It's been great to meet you all," said Alan. "Good luck, Lily—I feel pretty bad that Oz was kidnapped on my watch."

"You couldn't help it," Lily said.

"Oz is a very bright guy, and I've got a feeling he's going to be fine." He shook hands with Lily and Caydon, pressed Demerara's paw and drove away.

Lily and Caydon looked at each other.

"I didn't mean you were boring," said Caydon. "I just meant—I'm going to miss Oz."

"You can't miss him more than I do—I've never had to live without him in my entire life."

The front door of Number 18 opened, and there was Dad in his dressing gown. "Well, they warned us you'd be back at the crack of dawn! Hi, darling."

Lily hugged him, trying not to burst into tears again. "Hi."

"Hi, Caydon—would you like to come in? My wife's making toast."

"No thanks," Caydon said. "I'd better get home. See you, Lily."

"See you."

It was strange and horrible to be back at home without Oz—and extremely strange that her parents were so cheerful.

"I'm glad you had a nice time," Mum said happily. "And wasn't it great that Caydon was taking the same diving course? I was afraid you'd be lonely without Oz—but he's having a wonderful time at that music camp."

"Oh—good."

Music camp. That was where Mum and Dad thought he was.

"Have some toast."

"No thanks, they gave us breakfast."

Lily drank a cup of tea, listening to her parents chatting, slightly comforted by the warmth of Demerara's body across her feet.

"Drat, my nail polish has chipped!" The yowling voice floated up from under the table. "Be brave, Lily dear. We'll find Oz, and Isadore had better watch out—it's PAWBACK TIME!"

8

The Grotto

Oz felt a terror so intense that it blocked out everything else. He had been dragged through the murky
river water by a maniac in a white suit, sure he was
about to be killed. But the maniac had suddenly pulled
him out of the water and dropped him on hard pavement, and as soon as he realized he wasn't dead yet, Oz
began to pay attention to his surroundings.

His diving equipment was torn away from him.
While he lay panting and exhausted, he was gagged
and blindfolded, and his arms and legs bound.

"Keep quiet," a voice hissed in his ear, "and I'll let
you live."

He was picked up again and dropped on another
floor. Oz guessed he was in a truck or van. He could feel
the engine throbbing around him, and the van lurching
as it sped through the darkened streets.

Why wasn't anybody chasing them? Was Lily all
right? How were they going to explain this to his
poor parents?

The van lurched to a halt. Oz strained his ears for clues to where they were. He heard the door open and felt rough hands pulling him out. He was then flung over someone's shoulder.

After a lot of jolting he was dropped again, this time onto a carpet.

"I'm out of condition!" The voice was breathless. "That's what happens when you spend too much time in the lab."

Oz was untied, and his gag and blindfold removed. He struggled into a sitting position, shivering in his wetsuit and blinking in the light.

This was amazing. He was in a cavern, its roof hidden by thick black shadows. The desert of darkness was punctuated by little puddles of lamplight, showing groups of furniture like rooms in an invisible house. At the far end of the space Oz saw a laboratory gleaming with glass tubes and jars. One pool of light contained a carved wooden bed covered with a faded green quilt; another contained a white bathtub like a boat, half hidden behind a screen covered with pictures of castles.

The man he knew to be Isadore Spoffard sat in an armchair nearby, pouring himself a glass of whisky. Oz stared at the face he'd seen in the SMU mugshots, with its shifty dark eyes and thin black mustache. He looked about the same age as Oz's dad, but he had stopped getting older in 1938; how must it feel to be that ancient?

"Hello," Isadore said. "You're my great-great-nephew Oscar; how do you do. I'm sorry I had to kidnap you, but since I didn't get the mold I had no choice. I won't hurt you because I can't be bothered—unless, of course, you try to escape."

Oz found that he was a little less scared. "Where is this?"

"I call it The Grotto," Isadore said. "It's an old subway station—West Piccadilly—that fell out of use in the early 1930s. I came to live here after my official death."

"Why did you bring me here?"

"You're a hostage," Isadore said. "I'm going to swap you for the golden molds."

"Oh."

"This has been the most infuriating night. You have no idea how much time I've spent trying to get my hands on those molds! I knew perfectly well where they were—so near, and yet so far! Somehow their magic defeated me and I couldn't touch them. Tonight, I held Marcel's star, only to have it snatched away at the very moment of victory—" He broke off to sneeze violently. "I must get out of these wet clothes—and I suppose I'd better find something for you."

Isadore gulped the rest of his whisky and vanished

into the shadows. A few minutes later he emerged, wearing an identical—but dry—white suit. He handed Oz a small heap of clothes.

"Put these on and come out into the kitchen area, where I can make us some hot tea."

He vanished again, and Oz looked at the clothes. There was a pair of white linen trousers and a white linen shirt with long sleeves, both yellowed with age and far too big. He peeled off his wetsuit and made the dry clothes fit as best he could, rolling up the legs and sleeves. Isadore had also provided a striped tie, which he used to hold up the trousers. He was sure he looked ridiculous, but the clothes were soft and very comfortable.

To find the "kitchen area," he followed the sound of the old-fashioned whistling kettle, echoing off the tiled walls of the old tube station. In another puddle of lamplight was a glowing stove, a table and chairs and a wall covered with pictures—Isadore had made himself a surprisingly cozy home down here. Oz was interested to see, underneath the big lamp, a violin in an open case. He wondered if he'd be allowed to play it.

"I apologize for the oily smell," Isadore said. "I can't get electricity down here without being discovered. I make do with fires and oil lamps. Do sit down."

Oz sat down at the table and Isadore gave him a mug of tea, milky and sweet and delicious. It was not

drugged; neither were the ginger biscuits. As his bravery increased, so did Oz's curiosity. In his imagination,
evil Uncle Isadore had been a kind of monster, like a
Bond villain or an ogre in a fairy tale. In real life he was
an ordinary, sour-faced man, with a seedy air of loneliness and defeat.

"How long will you keep me here?" he dared to ask.

"I don't know. It all depends upon the man known
as 'J.'"

"I've met him."

"He has to give me my molds—so that I can at last
make my chocolate, and live out the rest of eternity as
the richest man on earth." Isadore poured more whisky
into his tea. "I'll fetch some food in a minute. There are
these very tasty newfangled things called 'pizza' that
I've recently discovered."

"Great," said Oz. He liked takeout pizzas and his
mother never let him have them.

"And there's a spare sofa you can use as a bed.
Frankly, I haven't really thought this through." Isadore
was gloomy. "I just grabbed you when I lost the mold.
I lost my head."

"They'll never let you make your chocolate," Oz said
boldly. "You might as well let me go."

"Certainly not. You're my bargaining chip."

It was depressing to be a "bargaining chip," and
horrible to think of spending any time in this ghostly

old tube station—but at least Isadore wasn't planning to kill him. Oz drank his tea and ate the biscuits. As he grew less scared, he began to pay more attention to the objects around him. Isadore's "Grotto" was crammed with antique furniture, old clocks, paintings and statues that made a net of weird shadows. Isadore shifted the oil lamp, and a face leapt out of one of the framed photographs on the wall—Lily's face.

A second later, Oz saw that it wasn't his sister, but a young woman who looked very much like her. She had the same bright black eyes, the same untidy heap of curly hair, the same dark freckles.

"Who's that?" he asked.

Isadore followed his gaze. "That's Daisy. She was your great-great-grandmother."

"Oh. I've only seen a picture of her when she was old. She looks just like my sister."

Isadore let out a long sigh. "Ah, my sweet Daisy!"

"You were in love with her." Oz remembered the long story Demerara had told them. "But your magic love chocolate didn't work."

"Yes, it did," snapped Isadore. "It worked perfectly."

"But not with Daisy."

"No—I was too late."

"She was already in love with your brother Marcel."

"All right! Don't rub it in!" All these years later,

Isadore was still in the agonies of jealousy. "If only—but she refused to eat the damned chocolate, and I was doomed to spend the rest of eternity ALONE."

Oz was interested. "Did you try to make Daisy immortal?"

"That was part of my plan." Isadore poured another slug of whisky into his tea. "But they poisoned her sweet mind against me, and she wouldn't trust me."

"Well, fair enough," said Oz. "You did kill her husband."

"She wouldn't have fallen in love with Marcel if she'd met me first."

"You don't know that."

Isadore winced as if Oz had stabbed him. "I DO! Daisy and I are destined to be together!"

"But she's dead," Oz pointed out. "She died before I was born."

"Daisy!" wailed Isadore.

To Oz's enormous embarrassment, Isadore began to cry. He pulled a handkerchief from his pocket and sobbed into it wretchedly. Very unwillingly, Oz found himself feeling slightly sorry for his wicked great-great-uncle. His wickedness had only made him lonely.

Isadore blew his nose, with a trumpeting that echoed forlornly through the empty station. "I haven't given up, you know."

"You—you haven't?" This was just plain crazy.

"Oz, I'll tell you something I've never told anyone." Isadore leaned across the table toward him, a hungry look on his thin face. "I have a dream—the only thing that has kept me from despair since my Daisy grew old and died!"

"You did tell me," Oz said uneasily. "You want to be the richest man in the world."

"But why do I need the money? Because my dream involves a very expensive spell. One day, I'm going to make a blend of magic chocolate that turns back time!"

"Oh."

"You think I'm crazy."

"Well, yes, I do a bit."

"If I had my way," Isadore said fiercely, "you and your sister and father would never have existed. My dream is that I turn back time to just before Daisy came to work at our shop in Piccadilly—so that I can kill my brother before she even meets him! Then we'll eat the immortality chocolate together, and live happily ever—EVER—after!"

"Oh." It wasn't going to be much fun, living with a man who wished you didn't exist. Oz would have been more worried, however, if he hadn't had a strange feeling that Isadore was rather glad to have his company. Maybe his best chance lay in being nice to him. "Is that your violin?"

"Yes." Isadore dried his eyes. "It's my only companion

in the long evenings. And it helps me to think. I play it when I'm studying, like Sherlock Holmes—you've heard of him, I suppose."

"The detective."

"I'm glad he's still famous. The modern world is a mystery to me." Isadore ate a ginger biscuit. "But I was forgetting, you play the violin. Please feel free to play mine."

"Thanks." This was a relief; Oz went nowhere without his violin, and he hated the idea of not being able to make music. He thought it a bit odd that Isadore knew he played. He knew an awful lot about the people he wished didn't exist.

"I can't force you," Isadore said. "Like the ancient Israelites, you may be unable to play your songs in a strange land. But it would bring me great pleasure to hear something now."

He was so hungry and sour and sad that Oz didn't have the heart to refuse. He went over to the violin and carefully lifted it out of its case. It was old and battered, the varnish covered with scratches, but it was perfectly in tune, and the tone was beautiful.

Oz played the andante of a Mozart sonata, and the music echoed plaintively in the great underground chamber.

Isadore wept again, and muttered, "Daisy—what other hope is there for me?"

Suddenly, Oz was more hopeful. The other voice that he and Lily had heard when they were little was weaving in and out of the music, telling him to be of good cheer. The magic had been with them all along.

9

Cat At Large

The house was spookily quiet without Oz and his music, and the day after the adventure in the river was as flat as a pancake. Lily tried not to mope too much, in case her parents started asking awkward questions. They were totally convinced that Oz was at music camp and having the time of his life—there were even two postcards from him on the kitchen bulletin board.

It would have helped to talk to Demerara, but there was no sign of her. Lily wandered from room to room, waiting for the appearance of the portly golden cat. She looked behind the metal cylinder in the workshop, hoping to see the magic door to the "flat," but the wall remained stubbornly blank.

"I'm sorry you miss Oz so much," Mum said. "But it might be good for both of you. Why don't you do something with Caydon? You got on so well at that diving course."

Lily didn't really want to do anything with Caydon. By the second day, however, she was so restless and bored—and so anxious to talk about what was really going on—that she went out into the street, where Caydon sat yawning on the wall.

"Hi."

"Hi," said Caydon. "Any news?"

"Nothing." Lily sat down beside him. "I think Demerara's up to something—I haven't seen her since we got home. She didn't even show up for her manicure."

"I suppose we'll hear if something happens," Caydon said. "I hope Oz is OK and not being tortured or anything."

"Thanks for cheering me up," Lily snapped.

"Sorry, I didn't mean to make it worse. Do you want to do something?"

"Like what?"

"I don't know," Caydon said. "Do you like computer games?"

"No."

"Swimming?"

"I've had enough of the water, thanks."

"Maybe you're right." Caydon thought for a moment. "What about skateboarding?"

"No!"

"Well, have you ever tried?"

"No."

"I'll teach you," Caydon said. "Come on—there's nothing else to do."

Lily sighed. "OK."

She fetched Oz's skateboard and began her lessons on the sloping path outside the flats. She kept falling off, but she was wearing jeans and not going fast enough to be hurt. After a surprisingly short time she began to enjoy herself.

"You're not bad," said Caydon. "Actually, you're already a bit better than Oz."

"Good," Lily said. "It's my turn to be better at something."

Caydon flipped his skateboard with his foot. "It must be hard work, having a genius brother. Are you jealous?"

"Not exactly—I don't want to play the violin. But I do get sick of always being the stupid one. At our old school they called us Pinky and the Brain—like the cartoon."

"Oh, I know," Caydon said. "One is a genius, the other's insane."

"That's the one."

"Look, you're always going on about being stupid." Caydon was serious. "But I think that must mean you're quite clever."

"Really?"

"My dear Lily, of course you are!" a yowling voice said.

"Demerara!" Lily cried joyfully. She bent down to stroke her fur. "Where have you been?"

"I've been studying Pierre's magic books in my flat. I've found a spell that will help Oz."

"Oh—that's wonderful! When can we do it?"

"Does J know?" Caydon asked.

For a moment, the furry face was shifty. "J doesn't need to know—I don't have to tell him every little thing!"

Lily was impatient. "Let's do it now—whatever it is."

"I don't want to get too technical," Demerara said, "but it's a divining spell—that means I will receive a signal that will lead me to Oz."

"Hang on," Caydon said. "If it's that easy, why didn't you do it when Oz disappeared?"

"Because it's COMPLICATED!" Demerara hissed. "I had to turn over my flat to find a certain magic cacao bean—it took me ages and my claws are RUINED! But I found it, and now I'm ready to do the spell." She opened her mouth wide, and they saw a long brown bean on her tongue. "I'm keeping it safe in my cheek. Come along, we've wasted enough time." She whisked round and trotted across the road.

Just as she reached the other side, a man walked past with a big dog on a leash.

The dog barked loudly at Demerara, who gave a shriek of fright—followed by a shriek of annoyance.

Lily and Caydon crossed the road to join her.

"Slight change of plan," Demerara said crossly. "I've

SWALLOWED the dratted thing! It was all that dog's fault."

Lily's heart sank. "Does that mean we can't do the spell?"

"Not now, I'm afraid. We'll have to wait until it comes out of me. What a nuisance."

"But—we don't have time! We have to help Oz!"

"I'm sorry, dear," Demerara said. "At least we know the bean is safe." She sat down on the pavement. "I feel slightly faint with hunger—someone get me a can of Whiskas!"

"I don't have any money," said Lily.

"I do," Caydon said. "I'll get it." Though he teased the uppity cat, he was fond of her. "What flavor would you like?"

"Chicken—or salmon, if they don't have that—goodness, how queer this feels!"

"Demerara?" Lily bent down to stroke her head. "Are you OK?"

The words died in her throat as she watched, transfixed.

The cat was growing. First she was the size of a panther, then a lion—and still her paws and claws grew, and her sharp teeth grew, and her mighty hindquarters swelled, until she towered over them, the size of a full-grown elephant.

"Good gracious!" Demerara cried. "I'm GIGANTIC— I don't look fat, do I?"

Caydon found his voice. "What've you done? What's happened?"

"It must be something to do with that magic bean. Let's hope I shrink back soon."

A young man stepped out of the supermarket. He gaped at Demerara, the color draining from his face. A moment later a woman with a baby buggy walked round the corner and let out a loud scream.

"She's VISIBLE!" groaned Caydon. "Now what do we do?"

Lily was still stunned by the sight of the giant cat—beautiful as ever, but suddenly more like a dangerous wild animal.

The dumbfounded young man dashed back into the shop. "Call the police!"

The woman with the baby kept screaming.

"Oh, what a silly fuss!" said Demerara. She had started to enjoy herself. "This is rather fun—I can see so much!" She stretched her head to peek into an upstairs window—a shout of terror came from inside.

"Look, what are we going to do?" Caydon asked again. "She can't stay here!"

Lily grabbed a handful of Demerara's fur. "Come and hide inside—I'm sure you can squeeze into the workshop—"

"She's too fat," Caydon interrupted. "She'll just get stuck!"

"I don't want to hide," said Demerara. "Why should I hide?"

A small crowd had gathered round them now. The woman with the baby had stopped screaming and was talking to the police on her phone.

"No, I am NOT seeing things! There's a giant cat on the loose!"

The young man was taking pictures with his phone.

After all her years in obscurity, the attention went to Demerara's head like wine. Her enormous furry face lifted into a smirk as she sauntered along the middle of Skittle Street. Every moment cars were stopping, and more people were appearing to stare at the elephant-sized cat.

"Come back!" Lily called.

"I'm just taking a little stroll, dear."

"It's a hologram!" someone yelled.

"It's a special effect from a movie!" yelled someone else.

The baby in the buggy laughed and cried out, "PITTY!"

"What a charming child," Demerara said graciously.

Lily broke into a trot to keep beside her. "Demerara, you can't show yourself in public—there'll be cameras and television and the police—"

"Television—really?"

"What'll J think?"

The monstrous cat stopped, crossly flicking her huge tail (it accidentally swept a traffic warden into the gutter). Her square green eyes narrowed. "He's such a spoilsport! But I daresay you're right—I'll try to squeeze myself back into the workshop."

"Good girl," said Caydon.

Demerara crouched down on the pavement. "Would you two like a little ride on my back? There's plenty of room for both of you."

"Oh, I'd love to—I'll feel just like Susan and Lucy in Narnia, when they rode on Aslan!" Delighted, Lily scrambled up the mountain of golden-brown fur onto the cat's broad back. It felt beautifully soft.

Caydon couldn't resist either. He climbed up behind Lily, and they both giggled when Demerara stood up.

"She's like a furry sofa," Caydon said.

"Are you comfortable, children?" Demerara purred.

"Yes," said Lily. "If you don't go too fast."

The cat's loud purring made her throb underneath them like an engine. She suddenly let out a cackle— and dashed out of Skittle Street.

Lily screamed, clutching handfuls of golden-brown fur to keep from falling off; Demerara's running was not as smooth as Aslan's.

"Stop!" Caydon shouted.

"This is very interesting," Demerara called over her

shoulder. "I can move so fast!" She smartened her pace until Lily and Caydon had to cling on for dear life.

The vast cat ran happily through the streets of Holloway. Cars screeched to a halt—a pale policeman tried to stutter into his radio—a group of skateboarding boys pelted after them with whoops of delight.

"Hey—it's CAYDON!" one of them shouted.

"Oh, do you know them, dear?" Demerara asked.

"Yes, they're from my old school."

She stopped suddenly and turned round. "Hello, boys—how nice to meet Caydon's friends."

The boys all roared with terror and dashed away as fast as they could.

"Now you've done it," said Caydon. "I'll never be able to explain this."

Demerara set off again, this time at a smooth trot. More people were gathering around them—at a safe distance. Loving the attention, the cat purred and smiled, and often slowed down for someone taking a picture.

It was like being part of a traveling circus, Lily thought; the traffic on busy Holloway Road stopped as the enormous cat made her stately progress, attended by a crowd that now included two police cars and a fire engine.

"Demerara, we really should go home—or at least get off the main road—"

"But I'm still very peckish, dear; I'll stop for a snack first."

"What kind of snack?" Caydon's voice behind her was alarmed. "You're not going to kill something, are you?"

"Oh, don't be silly—I'm not an ORDINARY cat."

"Come home and we'll get you something to eat," Lily said (frantically wondering how much cat food was in stock at the supermarket next door, and how she would pay for it).

"Hmm, I smell something tasty!" They had reached Archway, and the cat paused to sniff over the chaos of traffic, seething crowds and police cars. She trotted purposefully across the road.

"Where are you going?" Lily asked.

"Oh, no!" moaned Caydon. "Stop—you can't go in there!"

Demerara stopped again outside the Archway branch of McDonald's. She pressed her huge furry face against the window. The customers inside gasped and screamed, flinging their half-eaten burgers into the air and scattering fries.

"The door's too small for you!" Lily shouted desperately.

"Pooh," said Demerara.

Her furry back heaved and rolled, and Lily and Caydon were flung to the pavement.

More sirens were wailing now, and a helicopter clattered above them. Lily scrambled to her feet, rubbing her elbow.

Demerara held up one mighty paw and smashed a great hole in the window. She stepped through it and made for the counter, scornfully brushing aside tables and chairs. At the counter she stuck her head into the piles of waiting burgers and gobbled them down, paper and all. Right at the back, where the food was being cooked, she gulped down the raw and half-cooked burgers so fast that she almost bit the arm of a terrified employee.

Most of the customers inside McDonald's had escaped, and several were giving interviews to television news channels.

"Demerara!" Lily called. "Oh, this is a disaster! They'll shoot her with a tranquilizer dart and shut her up in a zoo—and we'll never find Oz!"

"Keep calm, everyone!" a voice shouted. "The situation is under control!"

A young policeman in full riot gear pushed his way through the crowd.

"Alan!" Lily was incredibly glad to see him. "What're the river police doing here?"

"The department's borrowing me from the river police," Alan said cheerfully. "I'm working on this case now—though I didn't expect it to get this interesting so quickly!"

"You're too late," Caydon said. "That cat's going to be all over the news."

"No she won't—that's why the SMU sent an emergency response unit." Alan pointed to a large black truck backing up against the curb. "We'll soon sort her out."

"What are you going to do?" Lily cried out. "Don't hurt her!"

"Don't you worry," Alan said kindly. He was carrying a megaphone, which he raised to his mouth. "DEMERARA—COME OUT!"

"No!" the huge cat shouted, with her mouth full. "Go away!"

"Lily, you have a go," Alan pushed the megaphone into her hands. "She might listen to you."

"DEMERARA!" Lily jumped with shock at the sound of her own voice ringing out across Archway. "PLEASE BE GOOD AND COME OUT!"

"Oh well," said Demerara, "I've eaten it all now." She let out a loud hiccup that rang out like a gunshot.

The mass of golden-brown fur turned, slowly lumbering back through the broken window to the pavement.

The SMU emergency response unit swung impressively into action while police in riot gear pushed the crowd back.

"Hello, Alan," Demerara said, her mouth full of

burger. "How nice to see you—what've you got there? OW!"

What Alan had was a syringe filled with blue liquid. He jabbed it into her fat golden-brown bottom, and the oversized cat slowly collapsed onto the pavement.

"You've killed her!" Lily gasped.

Demerara let out a loud snore as Alan and the other policemen threw a huge net across her and hoisted her into the truck with a special lift. With amazing efficiency and speed, she was packed up and whisked away. At the same time, the pavement under their feet began to vibrate, and their brains were invaded by a deep buzzing sound that gradually got louder and louder.

Gradually—and eerily—the excited mob of people subsided into silence, and a deep stillness fell across Archway. When the buzzing sound faded, they seemed to shake themselves awake. The people nearest to Lily and Caydon blinked in bewilderment and slowly began to move off. The television crews hurried back to their vans while the staff of McDonald's started to sweep up the broken glass as if nothing at all surprising had happened.

Lily grabbed Alan's sleeve. "Where have they taken her?"

"To be turned back into a little cat again," said Alan cheerfully. "A little cat—in very BIG trouble!"

10

The Phantom Busker

"Do you have ANY idea how much you've cost the department today?" the man known as J said sternly. "Do you know how expensive it is to scramble the memories of hundreds—thousands—of people? Not to mention wiping the pictures off their phones! What were you THINKING?"

"I wanted to find Oz without all the red tape," Demerara said sulkily. "I didn't mean to swallow the wretched bean—and I didn't know it would turn me into a giant. It's not my fault."

Lily wanted to stick up for her cat friend, but couldn't help thinking quite a lot of it had been Demerara's fault; nobody had forced her to parade through the streets in broad daylight and smash into McDonald's.

On the way to J's unofficial office in the MI6 building, Alan had driven Lily and Caydon to Muswell Hill. He had taken them into what appeared to be ordinary kennels, for dogs whose owners had to go away without them. Underneath the kennels, however, they had found a hidden network of huge cellars, filled with cages. Alan had explained that this was where the SMU kept all unexplained animals, and where they had brought Demerara to be shrunk back to her normal size.

There had been a reception desk, where Alan had to fill out a complicated form. While Lily and Caydon waited, they listened to the extraordinary noises around them—hoots, grunts and shrieks that didn't seem to come from any recognizable animal. The big cage nearest to them was empty, but something heavy could be heard trampling and shifting inside it. The sign on the door said EDWIN; the woman at the desk had told them he was a ghost elephant. Seeing Lily's face light up, she had kindly added, "Put your hand through the bars and he'll brush it with the end of his trunk—he's ever so friendly." And Lily had felt the soft, leathery touch of the ghostly Edwin; her mind was still full of him.

Demerara had been returned to them as a normal-sized cat, and she was in such a monumental sulk that she'd hardly spoken a word until they were shown into J's office for the official debriefing.

"Some guys from school saw me," said Caydon.

"They'll have forgotten all about it," J said. "I had to scramble the memories of every single person from Highgate to Islington, at hideous expense." He glared down at Demerara, perched on his desk. "You've been a very bad little cat."

Demerara's eyes narrowed to slits. "All right, I got a bit carried away."

"It mustn't happen again, do you understand? We're here to protect the public—not terrify them! Now get off my desk."

She dropped sullenly to the floor.

"We did try to stop her," said Caydon.

"You two did very well," J said. "And I wish I had more news to give you."

"Haven't you heard anything about Oz?" Lily asked.

"Nothing so far—we're combing every single SMU report for clues, and following up anything unexplained."

"But what if Isadore killed him?" Lily couldn't stop her voice from wobbling. "What will you say to our parents if he's dead?"

"Do you think he's dead?"

She thought about this—would she know? Deep inside she had always carried an awareness of Oz and his feelings, and this was still present, along with the other voice they had heard when they were little.

"No."

"Trust your instincts," J said kindly.

"Excuse me, sir." B62 put her head round the door. "Our agent from the London Transport Police has reported something odd—should I tell the desk to send her up?"

"It's probably nothing," J said, "but let's hear it anyway—and please bring some drinks in for Caydon and Lily. They've had a very stressful morning."

"And something for ME," said Demerara.

J's lips twitched. "And a small, cheap saucer of milk for this expensive cat."

"Yes, sir." B62 retreated quickly, trying not to laugh.

"For the last time, it wasn't my fault!" Demerara snapped.

B62 returned in a few minutes with a tray of drinks, and a wiry, tough-looking middle-aged woman with short gray hair, in the uniform of the London Transport Police.

"This is Joyce," J said briskly. "She was recruited after she caught some goblins in the act of messing about with the signaling."

"That's right," said Joyce. "The whole tube system's plagued with them—they're behind all the delays. Two of my colleagues were so shocked they had to go on sick leave, but I chased the little blighters out with a broom. Goblins don't scare me." She sat down and accepted a cup of tea. Lily and Caydon were given large glasses of Coke, and Demerara got a generous saucer of milk.

"You have something to report," J said.

"Yes, sir. I think we may have another phantom busker."

"Hmm, I suppose that could be significant." J noticed the blank faces of Lily and Caydon. "A busker is someone who plays music down in the Underground, and passersby throw them coins."

"They have to have licenses," said Joyce, blowing on her tea to cool it. "And we kept getting reports of the sound of a violin when there was no record of a licensed violin player."

"Violin!" gasped Lily.

"We searched everywhere, but the sound was always in the distance and we never found a trace of the musician," Joyce said. "So I thought I'd better file a ghost report. We have had phantom buskers before—there was a ghost with a tuba who was a right menace at rush hour."

Caydon's eyes were round with fascination. "Do you see a lot of ghosts, then?"

"All the time—the Underground's incredibly haunted."

"Oz plays the violin," Lily said. "It could be him, couldn't it?"

"It's not very likely, I'm afraid," J said. "But of course we'll follow it up. I'll arrange for you two to go on patrol with Joyce."

"An excellent idea," said Demerara. "If Oz is down there, they'll activate the magic. When do we start?"

"You're not going anywhere," J said. "You'll stay inside the house until further notice, do you hear?"

Demerara scowled. "Except when I slip outside for a breath of air."

"You won't be going outside at all."

"Wha—wha—?" The cat was puffed up with indignation. "You're telling me I can't go outside?"

"And if I hear that you've been outside without permission, you know what'll happen." J was very stern now—though Lily was sure she saw a glint of humor in his face. "You'll be taken straight back to the unexplained kennels—I'm not having this operation ruined by one naughty little cat!"

"Pooh!" hissed Demerara. "You are so UNFAIR! What about Spike?"

"Well, what about him?"

"Is he grounded too?"

"No," J said. "There's no reason to ground Spike—he doesn't have so much trouble obeying orders."

"Pooh and BUM!" The cat was furious. "You'll regret this! I'll go over your head! I demand to see Sir George!"

"He's been dead for thirty years," J said. "I'm in charge now—so kindly behave yourself." He smiled at Lily and Caydon. "You two kept your heads very well today; you make an excellent team. Well done and thank you."

Seeing that the important part of the meeting was over, Lily felt bold enough to ask about what was really bothering her. "Excuse me, but we saw—that is, we didn't exactly SEE him—but there was a ghost elephant."

"Oh, you've met Edwin!" J chuckled. "Yes, he's a dear old soul."

"Where did he come from?"

"When he was alive, back in the 1920s," J said, "Edwin was a very popular attraction at the London Zoo. He used to give children rides on his back; that's him on the wall over there."

Lily went over to the small framed photograph he had pointed out. It was a faded black-and-white picture of an elephant carrying several children in a wooden frame on his back. She stared at Edwin's friendly face, with its bright little eyes and smiling expression; it was incredible to think that she had felt the gentle touch of that long-vanished trunk.

"One of those children on his back is the real Christopher Robin," J said. "The little boy who owned Winnie the Pooh."

Caydon came over to look at the picture. "This place is so interesting—I'd really like to join the magic branch of the police when I leave school. How do I apply?"

"Just apply to join the force in the normal way," J said. "You're already on the record; you'll be put straight into the SMU, and sent to a secret magical training center attached to Hendon Police College."

"Cool!" Caydon was beaming. "I just wish I could go there now, and not bother with any more school."

Lily wanted to hear more about the elephant. "What happened to Edwin? How did he die?"

"He died of extreme old age," J said. "But it was obvious that his ghost was still in his cage. He was never visible, and he never scared people." (He shot a stern look at Demerara.) "So he stayed at the zoo until they needed the empty cage."

"Does he ever get visible?"

"One or two of our agents have actually seen him, but he's mostly happy to stay as he is."

Lily thought she would give anything to see the ghost of Edwin. Thinking about his kindly face was somehow comforting, and made her feel slightly less miserable about Oz.

It wasn't much fun being Isadore's prisoner, but it could have been worse. Oz spent the dark hours playing the violin and reading the old books and magazines that were stacked against the walls. Though he missed television and his computer, he quite enjoyed the prehistoric copies of the *Beano*.

Isadore mostly left him alone. He was working in his lab at the far end of his Grotto, filling the disused tube station with the rich scent of chocolate. He put all the chunks and squares of leftover chocolate in a huge bowl and told Oz to help himself. The chocolate was of the highest quality, but Oz quickly got tired of it. He also got very tired of the flat, damp, lukewarm takeout pizza boxes Isadore flung down in front of him every few hours.

After a few days (it was hard to keep track of the time down here), Oz plucked up the courage to ask, "Uncle Isadore, do you mind if we don't have pizza again?"

"I thought you liked it."

"Not for every single meal. Why don't you cook something down here? You've got the pans in the cupboard."

Isadore sighed heavily. "I was never very good at cooking and it's depressing when you're on your own. I've been living on fast food for years. It's certainly improved since the 1970s. How about Chinese tonight?"

"You could buy some food from a supermarket," Oz said.

"I haven't the least idea what to do with it."

"I could cook something."

"You?"

"I'm not very good at it. But I'd really like some pasta and tomato sauce, like we have at home, and I'm pretty sure I could make that."

"Really?" Isadore was eager. "Pasta would be a very agreeable change. Write me a shopping list—and don't try to escape while I'm out; I've sealed all the exits with magic fudge."

"OK."

"And please don't touch the fudge; it's vital for keeping out the goblins."

"The—sorry?"

"Nasty little beasts—why doesn't the government do something about them? If I paid any taxes it would make me very indignant. Do you promise not to escape? I'd hate to come back and find you gone!"

In spite of himself, Oz was touched. "I promise I won't try to escape."

"Thank you." Isadore hurried away into the shadows.

He was out for such a long time that Oz started to get a little worried. When he came back, he was laden with plastic bags from Tesco Express and Marks and Spencer, and his sour face was unexpectedly cheerful.

"I know this is more than you asked for," he said, "but it's been so long since I've cooked down here, I thought I'd make it an occasion. I bought a salad, a selection of cheeses and an amusing-looking bottle of wine."

"Great!"

"And I also bought you some new clothes."

"Thanks."

"I asked a woman in the shop what eleven-year-old boys normally wore—I must say, underpants are very colorful these days!"

Oz put on the jeans and sweatshirt, and they felt fantastic after Isadore's baggy, disintegrating cast-offs. After this, seeing that Isadore really didn't have a clue how to prepare the food, he took charge of the cooking. He heated water on top of the stove, cooked the spaghetti and heated the sauce, as he'd seen his parents do a hundred times.

Isadore laid the table more elaborately than usual, with linen napkins and candles in silver holders. He went to his lab to mix salad dressing, humming to himself—Oz wondered how many years it had been since he'd sat down for a meal with another person.

The food tasted excellent after a diet of nothing but pizza. Isadore sipped his wine and Oz drank red grape juice. Over cheese and chocolate, Isadore reminisced about his school days. "Mother wouldn't let us cast spells on our teachers, but I disobeyed and turned a ghastly old man called Mr. Frobisher into a goat . . . and then there was the time Pierre changed the soup into toffee, and everybody's teeth were stuck together until prep . . . and Mother smacked Marcel for growing toadstools on Father while he was asleep. . . . Dear me . . . happy days. . . ."

Oz had found that he could ask Isadore more or less

anything. "Are you ever sorry you killed your brothers?"

Isadore scowled, but looked more thoughtful than angry. "To tell the truth, I do miss them sometimes. We were very happy—until they betrayed me."

"Pierre didn't betray you," Oz pointed out. "Why did you have to kill him?"

"That had nothing to do with Daisy," Isadore said. "Pierre was furious that I used his mold without permission—he thought my immortality chocolate was wicked. When he found out I'd sold it to Heinrich Himmler, he most ungenerously hid all Mother's equipment." Isadore refilled his wineglass and cut another sliver of cheese. "Poor old Pierre—his trouble was that he was as wet as an August bank holiday. He had a lot of romantic ideas about using our chocolate to do GOOD—giving the stuff away for nothing!"

"So that's why he made the safe," Oz said.

"Yes—I don't suppose you'd tell me where it is?"

"No, of course I won't."

Isadore shrugged. "Worth a try."

"You're not trying very hard," said Oz. "Don't you have a spell that'll force me to tell you—like a truth drug?"

"I might have."

"Why haven't you used it? You haven't even made a ransom demand yet."

"I'll get round to it eventually. I'm not in a hurry—let's face it, I've got all the time in the world, and it's rather pleasant to have company."

"Oh." Oz decided not to push it any further. On the one hand it was a good thing that Isadore liked his company. On the other hand, he was longing to see his parents and Lily, and he did not have all the time in the world—he was starting his new school in a couple of weeks. How long would he have to spend as the prisoner of this nutcase?

"Goodness, that was tasty!" Isadore sighed. "And since you did the cooking, I'll do the washing up."

They finished the evening as they always did, with Oz playing the violin and Isadore weeping.

11

Underground Patrol

"Where do our parents think we're going today?" Caydon asked. "My mum just left me a note on the table, saying have a nice time."

"An outing to some Roman ruins," said Alan, from the front seat of the government car. "Organized by the local youth council."

"And where are we really going—the Underground?"

"That's right," Spike piped up. "We're joining Joyce for one of her patrols." He was perched on Caydon's shoulder. "I like the Underground."

"There are lots of rats down there." Lily was fond of Spike, but didn't know how Caydon could stand having the dirty little creature right up against his face. "I saw one at Goodge Street, running along between the tracks."

"Spike's the official Rat Liaison Officer," Alan said. "If it weren't for him, the whole Underground system would be swarming with hundreds and thousands of rats, like a moving carpet."

"Oh." Lily only just managed not to let this come out as "Yeuch!"

"Yeuch!" said Caydon. "I mean, I've got nothing against you guys personally—but that's gross."

The easygoing rat was not offended. "Yes—I've told them again and again, if the humans make such a stink about seeing ONE of us, they're not going to be very keen about a million of us! It's a case of give and take. They stay well out of sight, and the authorities go easy on the poison. Fair enough, I say."

"It's quiet without old Demerara," Caydon said. "I miss her."

"Me too," Lily said sadly. "I haven't seen her since we got back from the debriefing."

"She's furious about being kept inside," Spike said. "But she'll get over it—she'd never admit it, but she's scared of the Underground."

It was not a long journey; Joyce's office was at the nearby King's Cross Station.

"Very convenient because a lot of subway lines pass through here," Alan said. "And you've also got the railway and the Eurostar."

He parked the car and Spike hid inside his jacket while they walked into the busy entrance to King's Cross Station. Announcements boomed over the loudspeaker as crowds of people hurried about with heaps of luggage. Trains pulled in and out, and as usual Lily was confused by how ordinary everything looked.

They joined the fast-moving crowd going down into the Underground. Lily was bewildered by all the signs for different lines and destinations, and clung on to Alan's sleeve. On the northbound platform of the Piccadilly Line, he opened a small door set into the wall and hurried everyone through it while no one else was looking.

The light was dim now, coming from feeble bulbs set into the dirty tiled ceiling. They went down a metal spiral staircase that seemed to descend into the bowels of the earth. Every few minutes there was a great roar and a rush of warm, sooty wind as trains passed over their heads.

"Here we are." Alan opened another door, and they were in a clean, bright subterranean office with a flickering bank of computer screens. "Hi, Joyce."

Joyce, the tough gray-haired woman they had met at the debriefing, was filling a kettle at a sink in the corner. "Hi, everyone! Who's for a cuppa?"

Spike leapt off Alan's shoulder onto Joyce's head. She chuckled. "All right, mate?"

"Never better!" said Spike, hopping to the desk.

They all sat down and had cups of milky tea. Spike took occasional gulps of Joyce's instant coffee—which she didn't seem to mind at all—and nibbled at a lump of sugar.

"Right, I'll tell you what we're doing today," Joyce said. "The phantom busker was reported on the Piccadilly Line, so we'll be exploring that part of the system. If Oz is down there, you two will pick him up like a couple of television aerials."

"Do you think it might be Oz?" Lily asked.

"It might be nothing," said Joyce. "I wouldn't want you to get your hopes up too much."

Spike took a noisy slurp of her coffee. "I'll speak to a few of my connections—not much goes on down here the rats don't know about."

"By the way," Joyce said, "I wish you'd have a word with your lads at Holland Park—two sightings in one week, and it's a really posh station."

"They get careless," said Spike. "I'll put out another poison warning."

Joyce patted him affectionately. "I don't know what we'd do without you!"

When she (and Spike) had finished her coffee, Joyce opened a large cupboard. "Time to put on the protective clothing."

Caydon's eyes had been wide with fascination since their arrival at the station. "Why do we need protective clothing?"

"Because of the anti-goblin spray," Joyce said briskly. "It's very itchy for humans."

The four of them put white jumpsuits over their

clothes and had hoods that covered their heads and mouths. Joyce handed out large cans of aerosol.

"If you see one, don't think twice—give it a squirt right between the eyes!"

"How will we know?" Caydon asked. "What do goblins look like?"

"You can't miss them," said Spike. "They're about twenty centimeters tall, with enormous ears and mean faces."

"The little bleeders think train crashes are funny," Joyce said. "Squirt to kill."

"Cool." Caydon beamed as if he'd come to Disneyland.

Lily did her best to look brave, but her hands shook so much, she could barely hold her can of spray. She knew she couldn't kill anything.

"Chin up, love," Joyce said. "They hardly ever show themselves. Stick close to me."

The first part of the patrol was uneventful. Joyce and Spike led the way up and down staircases and along bare, badly lit tunnels. Joyce and Alan carried flashlights and carefully swept the beams around the walls.

At the top of one rickety spiral staircase, Lily suddenly caught a whiff of something familiar and unexpected. "I can smell coffee."

"Phew, me too," Caydon said. "Really strong."

"Coffee?" Joyce whipped round quickly. "Well done! That's a sure sign of goblin activity—they're mad for coffee, and forever nicking it from the shops upstairs." She shone her torch into a dark corner; Lily saw a heap of rubbish topped with a paper cup from Starbucks. "You two have great noses."

"Give it a good spray so they won't sneak back," Spike said.

Alan, who was nearest, covered the heap with a mist of anti-goblin spray.

They carried on walking, through long concrete tunnels just large enough to stand up in; Joyce explained that these were secret access tunnels, known only to the SMU and the Transport Minister. After they had been tramping along for nearly an hour, they stopped to rest and drink some more tea from Joyce's Thermos.

"Where are we now?" Caydon asked her.

"Underneath Piccadilly Circus."

Lily sighed and sat down with her back against the wall. "Is this going to get interesting at any point?"

"It's interesting already," Caydon said. "I can't believe I've been riding about on the tube with all this sort of stuff going on."

"My legs are tired." Lily had been hoping to hear Oz's violin, and was cruelly disappointed by the silence. "Ugh! What's that?" Something small and dark whisked past her foot. "A rat!"

She didn't mind Spike, but the idea of all those thousands of ordinary, mortal rats made her flesh creep.

"They're not supposed to use this route," Spike said. "But there're always a few troublemakers."

Two more shapes scuttered past, their little claws clicking on the tiles; Lily shuddered and hugged her knees.

"Hallo—" Spike dropped the lump of sugar he was nibbling. "Something's up! This could be a clue!"

Quivering with excitement, he jumped down in front of yet another hurrying rat. It was extremely strange to watch Spike talking to it in rhythmic squeaks, like something electronic.

The ordinary rat hurried off into the darkness.

Spike's whiskery face was thoughtful. "Something's up, all right—I couldn't get much sense out of him—he kept saying he was going to eat a big dead thing."

Caydon whispered, "Dead thing?"

"I'll get an emergency unit." Joyce was very serious; she pulled her radio out of her pocket. "Where is it?"

"In one of the old tunnels the rats are allowed to use," Spike said. "I don't like the sound of this—wish we didn't have the kids with us."

"They'll be safest with us," said Joyce. "You'll be brave, won't you?"

"Sure!" Caydon did his best to sound confident.

Lily was filled with a fear so terrible that she couldn't

put it into words—what if Oz had been murdered and the rats were rushing to eat his corpse?

Joyce took her hand. "No need to panic, love—ten to one it's a snoozing ghost, and they're too thick to notice." Her hand was warm and firm. Lily clung to it tightly.

"It's the old tunnel that leads into the disused station," Spike said. "Come on—we're not far away."

They set off again. Joyce muttered a few instructions into her radio. Spike perched on one of her shoulders, sometimes squeaking directions into her ear:

"Right here—door here—down these steps—"

The door at the bottom of the steps opened into a huge, black, windy nothingness. This tunnel had once been part of the Piccadilly Line.

Caydon hung back against the wall. "There won't be any trains, right?"

"That's one thing we don't have to worry about," Alan said. "It's been closed for years—which is why the rats are allowed to use it."

"What about ghost trains?" Lily asked.

"You're a sharp one," Joyce said approvingly. "As a matter of fact, we do sometimes see ghost trains—but only on New Year's Eve."

"Wow," Caydon breathed. "I thought I wanted to join the magical bit of the river police—but it might be more interesting down here!"

"What was that?" Lily gripped Joyce's hand. "Ugh—they're running over my feet!"

In the sooty gloom, the floor was moving. Hundreds of rats streamed through their legs; the walls resounded with squeaks. Lily was numb with the horror of it—those greasy bodies, with their scaly tails and hairy, pointed snouts.

"They're slowing down!" called Spike. "And I can hear lots of chatter about the dead thing!"

Even Caydon looked scared now.

"I don't think the kids should go any farther," Alan said. "Not till I've had a look."

"My backbone feels funny," Caydon said.

Lily felt a tingle of electricity; the magic pulled at them like a super-powerful magnet.

Alan shone his torch into a squirming, writhing heap of rats. The rats were swarming over something. Spike squeaked, and they scattered.

"Oh my g—" Joyce choked. "What the heck's that?"

It was a mound of fur the size of a small armchair—an enormous dead rat with two tails and six legs.

Lily was sick all over some nearby rats.

"I've changed my mind," Caydon said. "I'm not working in the Underground if I have to see anything else like that. Seriously, wasn't it the most disgusting thing you've ever seen?"

Caydon, Lily and Alan were sitting in a cafe in Muswell Hill, eating fish and chips. The disgusting creature had been bagged up and taken to the secret SMU kennel and the children had been sent off to have lunch while it was examined in the laboratory.

"It wasn't pretty," Alan agreed.

"Yuck, those two scaly tails! Wasn't it fat? And the extra legs! It looked like a big blob covered with dirty hair."

"I wish you'd stop going on about it." Lily's stomach still felt very weird. "It's putting me off my food—I think it's incredible that you can eat anything."

"I wish I'd taken a photo, that's all." Caydon squirted ketchup over his chips. "I'd love to show it to my friends."

"We've signed the Official Secrets Act," Lily reminded him. "You'd be breaking the law."

"I didn't say I was going to, did I? You're really in a grumpy mood today."

"And you're just treating this whole thing like a game!"

"I am not!"

"When my brother's missing—maybe lying dead somewhere—"

"Stop arguing, you two!" Spike's voice was muffled.

He was eating his chips inside Alan's pocket where no one would see him; rats are never welcome in cafes. "Alan—throw us some more chips, mate."

"OK." Alan dropped a soggy handful of chips into his pocket.

"What—no ketchup?"

"Back off; the chips are bad enough."

"Look—I'm sorry," Caydon said. "I know how serious this is and I swear I want to find Oz as much as you do. But I was having a really boring holiday before all this started—the guy I normally hang out with has gone to Cyprus with his parents. You can't blame me for being interested in all this magic and adventure."

"You can't help it," Spike said. "Because you're a witch."

"I'm not a witch, OK? Or a wizard, or a warlock or whatever. I don't know any spells and I still think there's been a mistake." Caydon was, for once, very serious. "But—did you get a feeling when we were in that tunnel? I mean, a feeling like we had in the sunken tram?"

"Yes," Lily said. "A sort of pulling."

"Well, I think it was a sign that Oz is still alive and kicking, and maybe somewhere near that old tunnel."

"Really?" Lily suddenly liked Caydon a lot more, and felt a little less freaked out.

"That's what they're looking for in the lab," Alan

said, slipping a piece of fish into his pocket for Spike. "Any sign of magic that will lead us to Oz. Come on, let's get back to the kennels. I want to know if they found any clues."

Lily didn't want to hear or see any more of the revolting creature they had found that morning, but what if its shuddersome corpse led them to Oz? Deep down, something was telling her to hope.

The moment they reached the SMU's secret kennels, she ran to the cage of Edwin the ghost elephant. It looked disappointingly empty.

"Edwin!" she called softly.

Caydon came to stand beside her. "He must be asleep—HEY!" He jumped back, giggling. "He tickled my neck!"

Lily stood very still. Something soft touched her cheek—the end of Edwin's trunk. She felt him grab a lock of her hair and give it a gentle tug.

"Ed's in a jolly mood today," the lady at the desk said. "He likes having someone to play with."

"Doesn't he get bored here?" Lily asked. "Wouldn't it be kinder to let him roam free somewhere?"

"Edwin doesn't want to roam free," the lady said. "He's a ghost, so he can go where he likes, and he happens to enjoy living in this cage—it was the only place he could settle in after he left the zoo. And we all enjoy having him around. He's our mascot."

Inside the cage, Lily heard something large trampling and shifting excitedly.

"Hello, Edwin." The man known as J came up to them, wearing a white lab coat over his suit. "How are you, old boy?"

He stood up against the bars of the cage, and the white handkerchief in his top pocket suddenly whisked into the air and floated above their heads.

J laughed. "He likes an audience." The handkerchief circled in the air and dropped softly on J's head. He stuffed it back in his pocket, turning back to Lily and Caydon. "The lab's had a look at that frightful thing you found in the Piccadilly Line. Among the contents of its stomach were fragments of half-digested chocolate fudge."

Caydon made throwing-up noises. "You had to look in its stomach!"

"Magic fudge," Lily said. "Isadore!"

"Yes, it's definitely magic," J said. "We think Isadore must have used it as a barrier to keep out intruders, and one fool of a rat managed to eat some. Spike!"

"Boss?" Spike's head popped out of Alan's pocket.

"Go and talk to your people. Find out EXACTLY where that beast first made an appearance. We have to trace the fudge before it happens again."

"Righto, boss." Spike climbed nimbly out of Alan's pocket and scuttled up to his shoulder. "We don't want huge mutant rats all over the place, do we? I'll soon get to the bottom of— ARRGH!" He suddenly shot up into the air. "What's going on? Put me down!"

The invisible ghost elephant had playfully grabbed Spike's tail with the end of his trunk. The shabby rat— still clutching half a chip in one paw—looked so funny wriggling in midair that they all burst out laughing.

"You're a very cheeky old ghost today," J said. "I think it must be because you like seeing Lily and Caydon—you were always fond of kids."

Spike landed back on Alan's shoulder. "Geez!" he panted. "Which way up am I?"

"When you've found the fudge," J said, "I want the whole area cleared so that we can send a specialist team in."

"I'll do my best, boss—but they're not going to like it. There's trouble every time you try to close one of our designated tunnels. You might get more rat sightings where you don't want 'em."

"Tell them we've opened another disused tunnel at the old York Way station. I realize it won't be easy for you, Spike—try to make them see how important this is. They could be helping to save London from an attack."

"Do you think we've found Oz?" Lily asked.

"Not yet," said J, "but this is our first real clue."

12

The Time-Glass

Oz and Isadore were having bacon and eggs, the other meal that Oz knew how to cook.

"Uncle Isadore!" His voice echoed in the empty station. "It's ready!"

"Coming!" Isadore's voice called back.

Oz set out Isadore's bottle of wine and his own orange juice. He had no idea how long he had been down here, but he had settled into a routine, as far as this was possible without daylight. And he wasn't scared of Isadore; sometimes he even had flashes of almost liking the twisted genius. His evil great-great-uncle told some fascinating stories, and though he refused to set Oz free, he was very good about buying things Oz wanted.

Thanks to Oz, he now owned a nonstick frying pan, some Handi Wipes and a set of new tea towels to replace the disintegrating old ones. Oz had even dared to tell him to buy himself some new clothes. "You didn't make your trousers immortal, and now they're falling apart."

Unfortunately, Isadore had no idea about modern

fashions. He had returned from his shopping trip with bright blue sneakers, green tracksuit trousers and an Arsenal shirt, and he couldn't see why Oz kept giggling at him. "These new styles are extremely practical, and so delightfully comfortable!"

He was wearing his Arsenal shirt now, under his tattered lab coat—he had been working hour after hour in a state of trembling concentration. "Bacon and eggs—how tasty! Will you join me in a glass of this rough yet amenable country wine?"

"I keep telling you—I don't drink wine. I'm eleven."

"Of course, of course." Isadore's pale face was almost cheerful. "But today we have something to celebrate."

"Oh." Oz somehow doubted he and Uncle Isadore would "celebrate" for the same reasons.

"Without being too technical, I've managed to blend plutonium-infused butterscotch with a powerful memory chocolate—and jolly tricky it was too!" He was highly pleased with himself. "It means that after supper, I can make a Time-Glass."

"What's that?"

"It's a spell our mother invented, for looking back at the past. Talking to you has made it all so vivid—I suddenly longed to show you everybody from the old days."

"Like home movies?"

"No, no—much better! You'll be able to feel the past as it happened—I can't wait to show you Daisy!"

"Oh." Oz was uneasy. This spell did sound interesting; he liked Isadore's stories about the firm's heyday in the 1930s. But what had become of his evil plan? "I thought you were making a ransom demand."

"That can wait." Isadore waved the question away impatiently. "You'll see that I was easily the handsomest— Marcel was weedy and Pierre was fat. At one time he tried to invent a slimming chocolate, but it didn't work and caused uncontrollable farting—good grief, how we laughed!"

"Uncle Isadore."

"I can show you in the Time-Glass."

"Uncle Isadore, you said you were working round the clock to get your hands on the other two molds and make your immortality chocolate. You said the Schmertz Gang had already paid you."

"There's no hurry. Now that I've got you, I can get those wretched molds any old time." Isadore picked up his glass and the wine bottle. "Come on, I want to play with my new toy!"

He led Oz through the clusters of dusty furniture to his lab at the very end of the old station. Oz had never been this near it; he stared round curiously. Isadore had installed a long bench and a large sink. There were shelves lined with jars and glass cases filled with gleaming metal instruments.

In the middle of the bench Isadore had propped up

a round silver tea tray (Oz now knew why Isadore had spent the previous evening polishing it). The surface shone like a mirror. A gas flame burned underneath a small pan of something bubbling and out wafted a powerful smell of chocolate.

"Sit on this stool," Isadore said. "I've diluted the mixture in almond milk; it's safest if you drink it."

"It's not dangerous?"

"My dear Oz, you know me well enough by now, I hope—I wouldn't dream of killing you unless I had to. Now drink the mixture." He poured the chocolate mixture into an egg cup and put it down in front of Oz. It now smelled of marzipan and Oz drank it in one gulp; it was amazingly delicious.

Isadore knocked back his egg cup. "Now hold my hand and stare into the very center of the Time-Glass."

Oz took Isadore's cold, bony hand. The center of the polished tray glowed with a silver fire he could not take his eyes off.

"I know—I know—" Isadore's hand was trembling. "December the twenty-first, 1936—my Daisy's first Christmas at the showroom—" With his free hand, he scribbled some numbers in the air. "Five o'clock in the afternoon."

At first, as the picture formed in the middle of the tray, Oz thought it did look like a two-dimensional home video. Gradually, however, the picture seemed to rise up around him in three dimensions, and though he never left his stool, he could feel the air of the past on his skin.

It was cold and he was looking through a brightly lit shop window, where three large Eastern kings rode on three magnificent chocolate camels.

"Wow!" gasped Oz.

"Yes, it was an eye-catching Christmas window that year," Isadore said. "It was my turn to design and make it, and I wanted to beat the chocolate Noah's ark Pierre had done the year before."

"You made this? It's wonderful!" The Three Kings were beautifully detailed, down to the tassels on their chocolate saddles and the curls in their chocolate beards.

"You really like it?" Isadore was pleased. "I must admit, I was rather proud of myself. Daisy said the camels had sweet faces."

"That's just what Lily would say," Oz said. "She can't eat chocolate animals. Did you get to eat these camels?"

"No, we always presented our Christmas displays to the Royal Family; if I hadn't turned evil I'd have a knighthood by now. Dear me—why haven't I done this for such a long time? I'd forgotten how busy we were that year!"

They seemed to melt through the festive window display into the grand and gleaming shop. Christmas garlands of holly and ivy hung from the ceiling, and the place was crowded with people in old-fashioned winter clothes—Oz saw the glass counter through a forest of hats.

Behind the counter, three young women in white caps and aprons and pink dresses carefully picked up chocolates with tongs and placed them gently into green boxes lined with gold tissue paper.

"Daisy!" sighed Isadore.

He didn't need to point her out; one of the young women looked exactly like an older version of Lily. It was weird to think this was how his sister would look when they were adults. Isadore stared at her with a drippy expression on his face, but Oz was more interested in the three men who stood at the back of the shop.

Here were the Spoffard triplets—three smart men in dark suits with waistcoats and gold watch chains. Pierre was the stout one, Marcel was actually rather weedy, and Isadore was Isadore.

"The other two girls were good," Isadore said, "but Daisy was the best—see how neatly she ties the boxes! Were there ever daintier fingers?"

The Isadore in the past was also staring at Daisy. Oz looked closely and saw Pierre's hand creep into his brother's pocket.

"Look—" he blurted out.

"The way she finishes the box off with a blob of gold sealing wax!"

Oz decided to keep quiet. In the past, he clearly saw Pierre take something (he couldn't see what) out of Isadore's pocket and hide it away in his own. Both in the past and present, Isadore was too busy gawking at Daisy to notice.

In the Time-Glass, the chocolate showroom was emptying. Oz watched the customers leaving with their exquisite boxes of Spoffard chocolates. The Isadore in the past looked at his pocket watch.

The present Isadore said, "In a moment you'll see me taking all the money into the safe—I had the responsibility because I was the oldest."

"Only by ten minutes," Oz pointed out.

"So? Ten minutes is ten minutes. Which of you two was born first?"

"I was," Oz said. "Mum told me Lily came out about twenty minutes later."

"That makes you the senior twin, just as I was the senior triplet. Everyone in the business respected my authority."

"I don't think Lily respects mine." Oz smiled to himself, thinking how furious his twin would be if he told her he was her "senior."

Isadore refilled his wineglass, intent on the sight of his former self taking bundles of coins and bank notes out of the till. "This is fascinating! I can't think why I haven't peeped into the past for so long."

Far away in the past, Oz saw Marcel and Pierre helping the three young women tidy the shop. While Isadore was bent over the money, Marcel quickly planted a kiss on Daisy's cheek.

"NO!" wailed Isadore. He swept his Time-Glass off the bench and the silver tray hit the wall with a tremendous clatter. "Now I remember why! Because I haven't found out how to change the past! And if I don't get the other two molds I'll NEVER find out!" He burst into noisy tears.

Oz was getting used to his great-great-uncle's outbursts and knew they were not dangerous; he would simply spend another night groaning and muttering, until he fell asleep among his empty bottles.

"You saw her, Oz—kissing my brother when my back was turned!"

"They loved each other," Oz said. "There's nothing wrong with that."

"It was disgustingly wrong!"

"Why don't you just—get over it?"

This was bold, but Isadore was not angry. "You'll understand when you're older." He wiped his eyes angrily with the sleeve of his lab coat. "Now play me a haunting melody, so that I can brood on what might have been."

"Well, OK—but isn't that a bit of a waste of time?"

"A waste of YOUR time," Isadore said. "I have all the time in the world."

"What about the gang?"

Isadore shrugged crossly. "You keep going on about those people—I'm starting to wonder if you're on their side."

"Of course I'm not—but didn't they threaten to kill you if they didn't get their chocolate?"

"They can't kill me. I'm immortal."

Oz was very tired of this argument. "They can destroy your work. How do you know they're not going to blow up this place? You'd hate that."

For the first time, Isadore's sour face was uneasy. "It's true, the boy's right," he muttered to himself. "I have all the time in the world, but that Schmertz Gang is impatient. Perhaps I should take the next step and make my ransom demand?"

Oz held his breath; it was a huge, vast relief to hear Isadore's first mention of his ransom.

Isadore drained his wineglass. "You know, Oz, you're a levelheaded boy. I shall be sorry to part with you—in another life I could have trained you as my assistant. But I have magic chocolate to make." He went to a drawer and took out an antique fountain pen and a handful of picture postcards. "Which one of these would you choose to write the demand on? There's a view of the botanical gardens at Ventnor—a picture of Bugs Bunny—a rather nice Turner sunset—"

Oz was impatient; this man couldn't even make up his mind about a postcard. No wonder he was such an unsuccessful villain.

"What about this one?" He pointed to a photograph of the Houses of Parliament. "Not too boring?"

"Uncle Isadore, get a grip—you can't send a ransom demand on a picture of Bugs Bunny! And Parliament's good—it might be the gang's target."

"My dear Oz!" Isadore was impressed. "When I do finally learn to turn back time, I'll be sorry to wipe you out of existence! That's an excellent notion." He unscrewed the top of his pen. "Though I believe their target is actually the Albert Hall."

"Oh." Oz kept his voice as casual as possible; he was pretty sure Isadore hadn't meant to tell him this.

Fortunately, Isadore was too busy frowning over the blank postcard to notice what he had done. "Now, what shall I put? 'Dear Sir'? 'To Whom It May Concern'?"

Good grief, Oz thought. "Why don't you just say what you want?"

"What about this—kindly return to me the two golden molds and the contents of my brother Pierre's—"

"Too long," Oz interrupted. "You want to keep it snappy—something like 'GIVE ME THE MOLDS OR OZ DIES.'" It was incredible that he was helping his wicked uncle to write his own ransom demand—but if he left it to Isadore it would never get done.

"Yes, very good!" Isadore said eagerly. "Admirably pithy and to the point!" He wrote the words very slowly and carefully and added something at the bottom. "HH 6781—that's the number of the hollow tree on Hampstead Heath where they can find my contact details." He placed the postcard in a saucer and snapped his fingers. The piece of card suddenly burst into flames and vanished. "You can't trust the post these days—I've sent it directly to Skittle Street."

13

Fire

"Hey—a fire engine," Caydon said as the government car turned onto Skittle Street. "I wonder where the fire— Uh-oh, it looks like your house!"

"What?" Lily gasped.

It was true. The front door of Number 18 stood open, the old metal shutters were blackened and bent and the pavement was awash with filthy water. Emily Spoffard was sitting on the pavement in a garden chair, drinking a mug of tea.

"Lily—please don't fly off into one of your panics," she said as soon as she saw her daughter. "There was a small fire in the old workshop, but the rest of the house is absolutely fine, apart from a bit of dirty water."

Now that the first shock was wearing off, Lily saw that the firemen were rolling up their hoses ready to leave. "What happened?"

"Well, I was sitting outside the back door, and there was a sort of *pop* like a balloon bursting. I didn't think anything of it, but a second later there was a knock at the door—it was your gran, Caydon. She was outside watering her plants when she saw black smoke seeping out of the shutters, and she raised the alarm before the fire had a chance to do much damage. Please say thank you—she had to go off to work before I had a chance— Oh, hello, Alan." Mum smiled at the young policeman. "What are you all doing here? I thought the kids were visiting some Roman ruins today."

Alan had been talking to one of the firemen, and his ears turned red. "I've been transferred to monument duty."

"It's very nice to see you."

"Can we go inside?" Lily asked. She was worried about Demerara; the workshop was her favorite sulking place.

"Yes—the firemen said it's just rather wet and smelly."

"Mrs. Spoffard, I think you should wait in the cafe for a few minutes," Alan said. "That'll give us a chance to mop up the worst of the mess."

"That's awfully kind," Mum began, "but I really couldn't—"

"No, it's a great idea," Lily said quickly. "Isn't it, Caydon?"

"What? Oh—yes." He knew as well as she did that this had not been an ordinary fire.

Mum agreed to go to the cafe, and Alan led the way into the filthy, dripping hall. He halted in the passage.

"That was a magic fireball aimed directly at the work-shop," he said quietly. "I'm willing to bet on it."

"We have to find Demerara," Lily said. "She must've seen everything—I hope she wasn't hurt."

"She's immortal," Caydon reminded her. "He wouldn't have killed her."

"I bet he tried!" Spike squeaked angrily, squirming out of Alan's pocket. "Oh, WHY wasn't I here to help her?"

"We'd better take a look at the damage." Alan pushed open the workshop door.

It was now a charred black cave of wet ash, and the metal tank in the corner had been blown into a few scraps of twisted metal.

"No sign of the old girl," Spike said. "She might be hiding in her flat." The rat took a flying jump to the floor, and the door to Demerara's secret flat was suddenly visible. Spike darted inside, and darted out again a second later. "It's EMPTY!"

"This could be tricky," said Alan. "Demerara's the only one who can tell us what really happened. We'd better find her so I can make a proper report."

They went into the residential part of the house, where the kitchen was covered with a lake of sooty water.

"Demerara!" Lily called. "Where are you? Demerara!"

She ran from room to room, looking under chairs and tables and leaving a trail of black footprints.

"Demerara!" Caydon called. "You can come out now!"

Upstairs, on the landing outside her bedroom, Lily heard an odd noise.

It was a quiet sound, a bit like hiccups. Lily realized it was the sound of a cat sobbing. She hurried into her bedroom. "Where are you?"

The sobbing went on, but there was no sign of the cat. Lily dropped to her knees and peered under her bed.

"Go away!" sobbed Demerara's voice. "Don't look at me!"

"What are you talking about?"

"I'm HIDEOUS!"

"Please come out, Demerara—I don't care what you look like—I'm just so glad you're all right!"

"Oh, Lily, what shall I do? I'm the UGLIEST cat in the universe!"

Alan and Caydon had followed Lily into her room. "I need to make my report," Alan said, "and you're the only person—er—cat who knows what happened."

"Alan? Are you here too?" Demerara cried. "Is the whole world to witness my SHAME?"

Spike scuttled across the floor toward her. "Don't be shy, old girl—you know you'll always look lovely to me. Why don't you come out?"

"They'll all LAUGH!"

"We wouldn't dream of laughing," Lily said hastily. "Would we?"

"Course not," said Caydon.

"Not you—those flowers!"

Lily cast a quick glance around the walls. The yellow roses on the wallpaper still looked like faces, but the faces were sweet and kind. "I promise they're not laughing."

"Oh—all right." Demerara sniffed and very slowly crept out from under the bed—a burnt cat, like a blackened piece of meat on a barbecue. She began to sob again.

Tiny voices rustled around the walls.

"Poor dear!"

"It's a shame!"

Trying not to cry, Lily gathered the charred animal in her arms. "That PIG Isadore! You poor little thing!"

Alan cleared his throat. "You don't have to tell me anything until you're ready. I'll go downstairs and make a start on the floors." He left the room, ears flaming.

"My beautiful fur!" wept Demerara. "My luxuriant yet easy-to-manage fur!"

"Now then, you silly old fart," Spike said kindly. "You know perfectly well it'll grow back, just like mine did after the experiment!"

"That's not the worst of it." Demerara held up a paw. "Look at my collar and bell!"

The silver bell was black, and the tartan collar was nothing but a few disintegrating cinders.

Caydon took the bell and he scraped it with his thumbnail. "I can clean this, and it'll be as good as new."

Demerara stopped sobbing. "R-really?"

"No problem—and you know, I've just remembered we've got a spare collar at my house; our cat never wore it. I'll go and fetch it."

"A new collar—what color is it?"

"Wait and see." Caydon grinned. "All I'll tell you is that it's the coolest cat collar you've ever seen."

"Thanks, Caydon." Lily had never liked him so much; poor Demerara was almost smiling.

"Back in a sec." Caydon hurried away to fetch the collar.

"What a nice boy," Demerara said. "Spike—how long did it take your fur to grow back after you were burned?"

"Not long."

"And—was it just the same?"

"Oh, yes," Spike said. "Your skin should've grown back by now, and the fur will start growing in a few weeks."

"Weeks?" Demerara's eyes narrowed. "Are you saying I'll be—bald?"

"Just for a bit."

"BALD!" The vain little cat began to weep again.

Lily gently stroked her burnt head (covering her hand with soot). "Let me wash off all this dirt."

"In WATER?" shrieked Demerara.

"Warm water—with rose-scented bubbles." Lily knew you weren't supposed to wash cats, but an immortal burnt cat had to be a special case.

"I suppose I could stand that," Demerara said. "Spike, you may go and tell Alan I'll be down in a minute, and ask him to pop next door for a can of Whiskas."

Lily took Demerara into the bathroom. She locked the door, in case one of her parents came in suddenly and found her washing an invisible cat, and ran a warm bubble bath. She lowered Demerara gently into the water, which immediately turned black. In the end, Lily had to turn on the shower attachment to remove all the burnt fur.

Demerara's hairless skin was the same golden-brown color as her fur. When Lily lifted her out of the bath, the plump cat looked like a bald, beige sausage. Lily wrapped her in a towel and washed out the filthy bath.

There was a knock at the door and Caydon said, "I've got the collar."

Lily opened it and whispered, "Don't you dare laugh—or she'll never tell us anything!"

Caydon's lips twitched at the sight of the bald cat, but he managed not to smile. "Here you are." He held out a collar of purple velvet, with Demerara's shining silver bell attached as good as new, just as he had promised.

Demerara's bald face was radiant. "It's WONDER-FUL!"

Lily fastened the collar around the cat's neck. "This'll look lovely with your new fur."

"Maybe you could come and make your report now," Caydon said. "Alan's waiting, and Lily's mum will be back in a minute."

"Yes, I can face him now—brrr, it's chilly without my fur!"

Downstairs, Alan had managed to wash off the worst of the soot and swoosh most of the water out of the back door; the ground floor was still wet and grubby but no longer covered with soot.

Spike, sitting on the kitchen table, jumped up when he saw Demerara. "Blimey, what a vision!"

"Great collar," Alan said. "OK—what do I have to tell the department?"

Demerara settled importantly on the table.

"Well, it was about half-past two in the afternoon and I was having a little rest in the workshop when a giant fireball suddenly exploded into the room. Everything burst into flames, including my gorgeous fur—everything except the postcard."

"Wait," Alan said, "what postcard?"

"The magic postcard that started the whole thing."

Lily jumped up. "What did it say?"

"Do you think I had time to read it?"

Alan was already running into the workshop. A moment later, he came back, holding a strangely undamaged postcard with a picture of the Houses of Parliament. "It's Isadore's ransom demand—I've got to get this straight to headquarters."

"At last!" Lily cried. "Now we can start rescuing Oz! Demerara—why didn't you tell us before?"

"Because I had far more serious things on my mind," Demerara said royally. "How was I supposed to think about anything except my lovely fur?" She shivered. "I've never been so cold in my life! Lily dear, could I borrow your pretty pink cardigan?"

14

The Video

"We've analyzed the postcard," J said, "and it's very much as we expected—fireproof and covered with an antitracking spell. That fallen oak tree over there is Isadore's hiding place—I'm just waiting until the area's cleared, in case it's booby-trapped."

They were on a bench in Hampstead Heath, beside a large pond that was busy with ducks and swans. All the joggers, dog walkers and mothers with baby buggies were being politely moved out of the way by the police—Lily heard one of the policemen saying something about a gas leak.

"How's Demerara?"

"Still moaning about her fur," Caydon said. "You know how vain she is."

"She's cold without it," Lily said, feeling she should speak up for her. "And she's really very sad. Every time she wakes up she checks to see if it's growing back, and when it isn't, she cries."

"And she's always nagging Spike," Caydon added. "I feel sorry for that rat sometimes."

"We'll see what we can do to cheer her up," J said.

Lily was thinking about the postcard. "Is there any clue to where he's keeping Oz?"

"Not yet, but I think we're just about to find out." J glanced around and went over to the fallen tree. Bending down, he rummaged among the tangled branches, and pulled out a small brown parcel. When he opened it, an old-fashioned plastic videotape fell out, and a note, with two words: "WATCH THIS."

Lily was excited, and very impatient. "When can we watch it?"

"All in good time," J said, smiling. "To tell the truth, I didn't really need you two here for the pickup this morning—I brought you for Edwin."

"Edwin! I thought he never left his cage!"

"He likes an outing sometimes."

"Where is he?" Caydon asked.

In front of them was the great, green sweep of Kite Hill, absolutely empty of people.

"Take a close look at the grass," J said.

Lily saw that the smooth, fresh grass on the hill kept going flat, as if being pressed down by an enormous invisible iron.

"He's rolling down the hill," J said. "It's his treat, but we obviously have to make sure he doesn't flatten any joggers or dog walkers—I mean, imagine being rolled on by an invisible elephant! Young Alan's keeping an eye on him—as far as it's possible."

"Oh, I wish we could see him!" Lily cried.

"SIR!" yelled Alan, halfway up the hill. "LOOK OUT!"

"He's rolling this way!" shouted Caydon. "He's going to roll into the pond!"

As they watched, the water in the nearby pond convulsed in a huge splash—as if something gigantic had been dropped from the air—and they were all drenched by a tsunami of weedy pond water. An astonished swan was swept into a bush, and the ducks went into a frenzy of quacking and thrashing.

Lily felt Edwin's dripping trunk. It crept around her waist, suddenly gripping her hard and whisking her off her feet. He put her down very gently, and then cheekily tried to push Caydon into the pond. After that he squirted them both with jets of water from his ghostly trunk, and the SMU "meeting" ended in screams of laughter.

"Sorry about the soaking," J said. "But Edwin had a wonderful time; you two have made an old dead elephant very happy."

"It was weird," Caydon said, "but brilliant."

"Edwin loves humans, doesn't he?" Lily thought how gentle the playful elephant had been with them.

"I'm glad you all enjoyed yourselves," Demerara said in an injured voice. "I spent this morning SHIVERING because I'm bald. Lily's cardigan is too big and it makes me look FAT. I might as well curl up and DIE—except that I can't even do that because I'm immortal."

They were in J's office in the MI6 building. After the soaking on the Heath they had gone back to Skittle Street to put on dry clothes (officially because they had fallen into the canal in Camden while canoeing) and had collected Demerara. She was wrapped in Lily's pink cardigan, with the sleeves tied up in a bulky bow, and her bald face was very cross.

"Before we watch Isadore's video," J said, "I gave your measurements to the clothing engineers. They came up with this; it'll keep you warm until your fur grows back."

He took something from his desk drawer: a little cat-shaped suit knitted in soft, fluffy mauve wool. Caydon gave a great snort of laughter—the suit did look comical—and Lily leaned over to nudge him; the last thing they needed was an offended Demerara.

She needn't have worried. Demerara beamed and her square green eyes were radiant. "For ME? Oh—it's divine! Lily, help me put it on!"

Lily took the little suit, and spent quite a long time

squeezing it over the cat's round bald stomach; it was very tight-fitting and clung to Demerara like a second skin.

"So soft and warm—and the color! Lift me up to the mirror, dear."

There was a large mirror on the wall, above a sideboard. Lily lifted Demerara up to gaze at herself admiringly. The knitted suit had holes for her ears; otherwise even her tail was covered in mauve wool, and she looked like a cuddly knitted toy.

"It tones so well with my new collar!"

"We ought to watch the video now," J said.

Demerara gazed at her reflection. "What about refreshments?"

"Don't worry." J hid a smile. "I haven't forgotten."

B62 came in with a large plate of sandwiches and a small bowl of fancy cat food. The picture of the queen behind J's desk turned into a white television screen, which suddenly flickered to life.

"OZ!" Lily started out of her chair at the sight of her brother's face, looming into the camera.

"Right," Oz said, "it's recording properly now." His face vanished.

The screen was now filled with the peevish features of Isadore, against a background like a junk shop, cluttered with furniture and knickknacks. "You're sure? Will they be able to hear me?"

"Yes!" whispered Oz's voice. "Just talk normally."

"Ahem," said Isadore. He glared into the camera. "Hello. You know what I want. Give me the molds, or— what was it?"

Oz's voice whispered, "Or you'll be forced to kill me."

"Oh, yes! Give me the molds! I have Oscar Spoffard, and if you disobey me I will be forced to kill him." Isadore looked away from the camera. "Should I do an evil laugh at this point?"

"No!" hissed Oz. "Get on with it!"

"I think I should be standing up—and you should be standing beside me."

There was some muttering, impossible to make out. The screen went blank for a moment. When the video continued, Isadore stood with one hand resting on Oz's shoulder.

"Listen carefully," Isadore said. "You won't get the boy until I get the two chocolate molds that once belonged to my brothers Pierre and Marcel. When I've established that they're genuine and not copies, I will send another message explaining where to find him. In the meantime, you will place the two golden chocolate molds at the very top of the Albert Memorial in Kensington Gardens. I must warn you that I will be heavily protected—your hidden cameras and infrared beams will be useless. How do you know I'll keep my word? You DON'T! But if you want to see this boy alive again—" He glanced at Oz. "You'll just have to trust me."

He stood very still for a few seconds, and added, "That went quite well; I don't think I'll go for another 'take.' But I still think I should have done my evil laugh."

"Over the top—always leave them wanting more." Oz walked toward the camera, and the screen went blank.

Lily was light-headed with the relief of seeing that Oz looked and sounded perfectly normal, even quite cheerful. "He's fine, isn't he? He didn't look as if he'd been tortured."

"He seems to be getting on quite well with Dr. Evil," Caydon said.

"Ugh, horrid man." Demerara sniffed. "And what on earth is he wearing?"

"An Arsenal shirt—so he must have some good points."

"When will I see Oz? Are you putting the molds wherever he said?" Lily asked, suddenly longing to be with her twin.

"Certainly not," J said briskly. "We do not negotiate with gangs."

"But—but Isadore will—will—hurt him!" She couldn't bring herself to say the word "kill."

The intercom buzzed; "Joyce is here, sir; shall I show her in?" B62 said.

"Yes, at once." J smiled at the children. "I think this is what we've been waiting for."

"Hi, kids!" Joyce came in, grinning all over her leathery face.

Spike sat on her shoulder, whiskers bristling triumphantly. "Don't go mad or anything—but I think we've found the old bum's hideout!"

"WHAT!" If Isadore's hideout had been found, Oz would be rescued—maybe even today. Lily's heart leapt with hope.

Joyce placed a plastic bag on J's desk. "Here's the proof: the same magic fudge we found in the stomach of the mutant rat."

"It was right down the end of a tunnel that had been bricked up," Spike squeaked. "The rats had worked the bricks loose, and that's how Mr. Two-Tails got in."

"Excellent," J said. "Well done, both of you. Were there any more mutants?"

"Just one gigantic slug," Spike chuckled. "Yeuch—it was no oil painting, let me tell you! That's one dead thing even rats won't touch."

"We're now trying to find out what's behind the fudge barrier," said Joyce. "And if that doesn't lead us straight to Isadore, I'll eat my anti-goblin spray!"

15

Flight

"Well, that was a waste of time!" Isadore appeared suddenly (Oz could never tell exactly where he came from), looking very annoyed. He was wearing a blue suit that Oz had never seen before, which was hanging off him in muddy ribbons. "I cleverly disguised myself as a traffic warden and went all the way to that tasteless Albert Memorial, and I couldn't get near it! They'd booby-trapped it by surrounding it with a crowd of ghosts—as if I wouldn't notice them!—and ignored my ransom postcard."

"I told you it was unrealistic." Oz put down the ragged old comic he had been reading and took Isadore's plate of fish fingers, mashed potatoes and peas from where it had been keeping warm on top of the stove. "I saved you some."

"Good—I'm famished! Pass me my bottle of wine."

"Get it yourself," Oz said. "I'm not going to help you to get drunk."

"My dear Oz, you're forgetting that I'm immortal. I

CAN'T drink myself to death—do you think I haven't tried?"

"You can't die, but you can say the same things over and over again."

"I don't care; I need something after that ordeal." Isadore fetched his bottle of wine and his glass and sat down at the table. "Just as I was slipping away one of the wretched ghosts spotted me—there I was being chased across the park by a crowd of government phantoms. I dashed into the road and the ghosts scampered when I was knocked down by a bus. Then of course there was no way out of it—I couldn't explain why I wasn't dead and I had to jump out of the ambulance and run like blazes. My only consolation is that it'll cost the SMU an absolute fortune to erase everybody's memories. It was all most upsetting."

"I keep telling you," said Oz, "you won't get the molds unless you set me free."

Isadore shrugged crossly. "Why does everyone have to be in such a hurry? Since you've finished your supper, you can play me that charming Bach chaconne you've been working on."

Oz had grown very fond of Isadore's violin, with its beautiful, haunting voice. He picked it up and began to play while Isadore ate his fish fingers and—as usual—softly wept.

Through the music Oz thought he heard something. He stopped playing.

"Why have you stopped?" Isadore demanded.

"That sound—didn't you hear it?"

"No."

"Sort of tapping."

They were both quiet. This time, they both heard it—a distant chipping or scraping.

"My fudge barrier!" Isadore jumped out of his chair. "Could they have found me?"

Oz put down the violin, his heart knocking against his ribs. This might be the SMU come to rescue him, and he was weak with longing for home—but he couldn't help a pang of sympathy for Isadore.

Suddenly a hand gripped his throat, and something cold and metallic was shoved against his windpipe— through his shock, he saw Isadore's mouth fall open in absolute horror. It all happened so quickly that it took Oz several minutes to register that they had been invaded by a strange man who was holding a gun to his head. He was so terrified that he was almost calm.

Isadore's sallow face had turned gray. "Let the boy go."

"No," the stranger said. "I'm holding this boy until you give me the chocolate that will make me immortal. Where is it?" He was about the same age as Oz's dad, with brown hair, pale skin and a slight American accent, and he could have come from anywhere. He was dressed all in black and the handle of another gun stuck out of the pocket of his black leather jacket. "If you don't hand it over, I'll kill the boy."

"Please!" gasped Isadore. He made a visible effort to calm himself. "You should have told me you were coming."

"So you could bake a cake?" The man let out a sneering laugh and his fingers bit into Oz's throat. "I don't trust you, Spoffard. We paid you and you disappeared."

"I—I came to all the meetings, didn't I?"

"Listen to me, you broken-down old drunk—all my plans depend on me being impossible to kill! Give me the chocolate!"

"I—we were just finishing it—weren't we, Oz?" He shot a pleading look at Oz.

"Y-yes—" Oz managed to say, though he knew Isadore was lying.

"The boy is my assistant," Isadore said. "If you don't let him go, I can't finish your chocolate."

There was a tense silence. "Nothing was said about an assistant," the stranger said.

"Naturally, I can't do everything alone." Isadore was getting braver. "He's my nephew, and essential to the whole operation. I really must insist that you let him go."

The stranger suddenly shoved Oz across the kitchen space toward Isadore. "Get on with it!"

Isadore grabbed Oz. "You're very welcome to watch us at work."

"That is just what I intend to do."

"Would you care for a glass of wine?"

"No."

"As you wish. Come along, Oz—let's get back to the lab."

Doing his best to look casual, Oz followed Isadore to the laboratory at the end of the disused station. The stranger walked close behind him. He sat down on a high stool, pointing his gun at Oz and Isadore. There was a deadly atmosphere around him that made Oz more seriously frightened than he had ever been in his life.

Isadore put on his white coat, handed another white coat to Oz, and bustled about the cabinets and drawers pulling out tools and molds and canisters of ingredients. His hands were shaking; his thin face was gray with fear, but he kept his voice steady.

"Oz, pass me that little black velvet bag."

Oz passed him the bag. Isadore opened it and a faint silvery light seemed to concentrate around the object he pulled out—his golden chocolate mold, carved with the face of a smiling moon.

"You said there were three of those," snarled the stranger. "Where are the other two?"

"Well—er—I've already used the others, and this is the last one."

"Oh—hurry up, then."

Oz drew a deep breath and forced himself to be calm. The stranger believed this lie, and that showed he knew nothing about the magic. Isadore was putting on an elaborate act for him—but how long could he keep it up?

Isadore set the precious golden mold on a matching golden stand. Oz had never seen him using it—he had explained that it was reserved for the very strongest magic. He put a silver bowl over a pan of boiling water, threw in some squares of plain chocolate and told Oz to stir it gently while it melted.

"How much longer is this going to take?" the stranger snapped.

"Nearly there." Isadore sprinkled a pinch of dark red crystals into the melting chocolate. While he bent over Oz, he whispered, "Don't breathe the fumes!"

"Get on with it!"

"I'm sorry, this kind of magic can't be hurried. If you don't mind my asking—how did you find me?"

The stranger grinned nastily. "You're not the only magic guy on the payroll."

"What?" Isadore was alarmed. "What do you mean?"

"You were seen buying underpants in Marks and Spencer. We followed you into the tube and our other magic guy did the rest. He's a goblin."

Oz stirred the smooth, glossy melted chocolate; the

word "goblin" made this seem even more like a bizarre and terrible dream.

"Drat!" Isadore, pale and breathing hard, opened a small jar labeled "Spider's Legs" and shook a few into the chocolate. "Those little beasts! I'm surprised you trusted him."

"Oh, I OWN this goblin," said the stranger, with a wolfish grin. "There's been another split in the group; I paid this goblin to tell me where you were first, so I could get a jump on the breakaway faction—no way will *they* get to live forever!"

"Good grief," Isadore said. "You people are constantly falling out—I hope you don't do it when you're immortal, or where will it all end?"

"Cut the chitchat!"

"It's done." Isadore was deathly pale. "The chocolate will be ready as soon as it's molded and set—it sets very quickly."

"Good," the stranger said, "but how do I know it's the right stuff? How do I know you haven't poisoned it?"

"I shall eat some myself."

"You're immortal—no amount of poisoned chocolate could kill you. Make the boy eat some."

"Oh, but surely that won't be—"

"Make the boy eat it!"

"All right, no need to make a fuss, of course he'll eat

some." Isadore dipped a silver teaspoon into the fragrant melted chocolate and held it out to Oz, with a look in his eyes that Oz didn't understand. What was he being asked to swallow? Never mind—he had a strong sense tht his wicked great-great uncle was on his side. He gulped down the spoonful of chocolate.

Isadore and the stranger watched him intently.

The delicious taste on Oz's tongue slowly spread down his throat and into his chest, stunning him into a sweet stupor. He gripped the edge of the workbench, wondering why he was so light-headed.

"OK, OK," the stranger said. "He hasn't turned green or dropped dead, don't waste any more of the stuff."

"If you're satisfied, I'll pour it now." Isadore moved Oz aside to pick up the bowl of chocolate. "Where's my gold scraping trowel?"

Very slowly, he poured the chocolate into his magic golden moon mold. Through his wooziness Oz was sure he saw a minuscule grain of something in the gold trowel, before Isadore began using it to scrape the bowl. With the stranger watching hungrily, he held both his hands over the mold. There was a short, sharp gust of cold air. He gave the golden mold a gentle tap against the bench and turned out a perfect chocolate full moon.

The stranger's eyes lit up greedily. He snatched the chocolate and took a savage bite. "I can feel it working!

The taste is taking my senses by storm! I'm IMMOR-
TAL!"

Isadore had stopped trembling, though he
was still very pale. "It feels good, doesn't it?"
The stranger gave a bark of laughter. "Fantastic!"

"Do you feel it in your arms yet?"

"Yes—and my legs! And now my whole head is filled
with fireworks!"

"That means it's working," Isadore said quietly. "I'm
so glad."

The stranger said nothing.

"Thank goodness you're a fool and you don't know
when you're being double-crossed!" Had Isadore lost
his mind? Even with a swimming head, Oz was horrified by this reckless piece of rudeness—but the stranger
said nothing.

Isadore put his finger to his lips and studied his
watch. After about thirty seconds of silence—which
seemed to Oz to stretch on and on—he walked over to
where the stranger was sitting and boldly gave him a
poke in the ribs. The man did not move; he was a grinning statue clutching a gun.

"Thank goodness!" Isadore collapsed into a chair,
mopping his brow with a chocolate-stained handkerchief. "I thought he was going to shoot you—I'd forgotten how dreadful it feels to be afraid for someone else!"

"What've you done to him?" Oz whispered.

"Killed him," Isadore said. "He's as dead as a door-nail."

"Oh." Oz looked fearfully at the still, silent stranger; he had never seen a dead person before, and it made him slightly sick that Isadore could talk so casually about killing someone. But he knew that his great-great-uncle had done it to save him. "What do we do with him now?"

"Never mind him!" Isadore jumped to his feet. "We have to get out!"

Oz watched, bewildered, as Isadore dragged a dusty, scuffed leather case from a nearby heap of clutter and started throwing things into it—jars, bottles, tools, notebooks, clothes, tins of food and thick rolls of cash, all in a chaotic heap. He snatched the photograph of Daisy off the wall, hastily wrapping it in an old vest.

"Uncle Isadore, what's going on?"

"My cover's blown—if this idiot fell out with the other gang members they'll be right behind him—and goodness knows what government forces will be behind THEM! There's not a moment to lose!" Isadore put the golden mold back into its black velvet bag. "Where to go next—that's the big question—where NOBODY will find us!"

Oz's head was very light now; a mist was creeping up around him, and Isadore's voice came from a long way off.

"Forgive me, Oz—I had to make you eat some but I swear I left out the poison!"

He felt himself sinking into the mist. There was a deafening explosion—and then the light went out completely.

"

16

The New Tutor

"Her name's Janice Hardy," Dad said, shutting his briefcase, ready to go out. "I haven't actually met her, but she sounded very nice—young and a bit shy, but obviously an excellent teacher."

"I don't want another tutor." Lily thought it was hugely unfair that she had to worry about writing and math when she was already so worried about Oz.

"Try to make her feel welcome, Nutella—you might even like her."

"OK, but I'm not doing piles of stupid homework."

"She said she'd be here at ten." As usual, Dad wasn't listening properly. He kissed Mum, pinched Lily's cheek and left the house whistling cheerfully.

Lily went upstairs to her bedroom. Demerara, in her mauve knitted suit, was sitting in the middle of the duvet.

"I don't like it, Lily."

"Don't like what?"

"Spike's not back yet. He went out yesterday afternoon and I haven't seen him since."

"Hmm?" Lily straightened a row of colored pencils on her desk.

"He's never stayed away this long—not in all the years I've known him."

Lily looked properly at her cat friend and saw that her bald, beige face was creased with anxiety; Demerara was a lot fonder of Spike than she let on. "Do you know where he was going?"

"I never ask Spike where he's going," Demerara said, "because it's often somewhere revolting and I'd rather not know. But what could've happened to him?"

"He might be doing something for the department." Lily sat down beside her on the bed and stroked her woolly back. "And you know he can't be badly hurt or dead. He's immortal."

"Lily!" Mum called from downstairs.

"My new tutor's here," Lily said, sighing crossly. "They just won't listen when I say it doesn't do any good."

"I'll come down with you." The plump mauve shape jumped off the bed.

"OK—but don't talk too much, or I'll forget you're invisible and answer you, and then she'll think I'm bonkers."

In the sunny kitchen, Mum was having tea with a stranger. "Hi, Lily," she said brightly. "This is Janice."

"Hi," Lily said faintly.

"Oh my gracious golliwogs," Demerara said. "What have we here? I don't want to be mean, dear—but she looks like a weight lifter."

Lily nearly cried out "Demerara!" and managed to turn it into a cough at the last minute.

Janice Hardy was a great, strapping woman in leather trousers and jacket, with cropped red hair, a surly face and a jutting jaw. She stared at Lily with eyes like sour brown currants.

Mum did not seem to notice anything wrong with this horrifying person. "Lily's reading is getting much more fluent," she was saying. "And she's found the spell check on the computer extremely useful when it comes to writing. It's the math we're having a real problem with. What method of teaching do you favor?"

The new tutor drained her mug of tea in one slurp. "Venn is your husband coming back?" She had a deep, croaky voice with a strong foreign accent.

"My husband?" Mum was bewildered for a moment. "Well, not until about six. He's very keen on giving our daughter more confidence in her own intelligence."

"And zere is access to ze street from ze garden?"

"Er—no, we back onto the garages in Pooter Lane."

Lily's spine tingled and her every hair stood on end; this woman reeked of menace.

"I don't like her," Demerara said. "She's not magic—

she can't see or hear me, any more than your poor mother can—but I don't like her one little bit."

She trotted over to take a closer look—and jumped as if she'd had an electric shock.

"More tea, Janice?" Mum asked. "And then you can settle down to work in the sitting room."

"Lily, dear," Demerara said. "Don't look up or down, just listen to me very carefully. That woman is carrying a gun. I may not know much about humans, but I do know that it's not normal for a tutor to be armed."

It took every particle of willpower not to shriek; Lily knew she had to keep calm.

She felt Demerara's warm body rub against her leg.

"You must make an excuse to nip out of the house for a few minutes."

Lily's mouth was dry; she didn't like leaving her mother with this suspicious character, but she couldn't argue. She stood up and made an almighty effort to look bright and normal. "Oh—do you mind if I just pop over to Caydon's before we start our lesson? I promised to lend him—er—Oz's skateboard."

"All right, if you're quick," Mum said. "Janice and I can have another cup of tea and get to know each other."

"NOW, dear!" mewed Demerara.

Lily stood up, on legs that felt like jelly, and made for the kitchen door. Somehow she got out into Skittle Street without bursting into tears of terror. "What now?"

The mauve cat was already leading the way across the road. "We're going to Caydon's."

Lily knocked loudly on the purple front door. For what seemed like ages (but was only a few seconds) nothing happened; a loud television could be heard from the sitting room in the back.

"Hi, Lily." Caydon opened the door eating a piece of toast. "What's up?"

"My tutor's got a gun!" Lily blurted out, and began to cry helplessly.

"I'll contact the SMU," Demerara said. "You must call the police."

"The normal police?" Caydon was baffled. "What am I meant to tell them?"

"This isn't magic, dear—tell them there's a woman with a gun, and a hostage situation at 18 Skittle Street."

"WHAT?" He stared at Lily.

"I swear she's not making it up."

"You'd better come in," Caydon said. "Come into the kitchen—it's Gran's day off and she's watching TV in the sitting room."

The kitchen was small and cheerful, and reassuringly ordinary. Demerara took charge. "You can make the call to the police, Caydon. Make sure you tell them about the gun. I'll just slip out to make my emergency report to the department."

"Slip out where?" Lily asked.

"Oh, I'm not going far." Demerara had her shifty look. "I shan't be a minute." She trotted out of the room.

"Well, what a day it's been," Mum said. "Who'd have thought that nice Janice was an international spy? Apparently the real Janice Hardy was found tied up in a cellar, poor thing."

"I'm sorry I missed all the hoo-hah," Dad said. "I'd like to have seen that police helicopter! And I hate to think of you going through it alone."

"It was fine—Lily popped across the road, and the next thing I knew, two huge armed policemen were wrestling that woman to the floor. I must say, they were very polite and full of apologies." She smiled at Lily. "They said you were a heroine."

"I didn't do anything," Lily said.

Dad ruffled her springy hair. "You somehow knew you had to call the police; that was pretty amazing."

"I—I saw the gun under her jacket."

"You were a star," Mum said. "You deserve to have a lovely time at this camp of yours—when are they coming for her, Bruce?"

This was the first Lily had heard about any camp, but she wasn't surprised; she might have guessed the SMU would want her for another assignment after today's near disaster.

"You'll have plenty of time to pack after supper," Dad said comfortably. The three of them were eating lasagne and salad around the kitchen table.

"I've already done most of it," Mum said. "It won't take you long to finish it off."

"It's going to be horribly quiet for us," Dad said, "with both of you gone."

Lily swallowed the lump that rose in her throat. Where was Oz? Where was she going, and how long would it be before she saw her parents again? Suppose the new baby was born while she was away? Lily was dying to see the new baby.

But none of this could be said to poor, innocent Mum and Dad, who were so creepily calm and jolly that Lily was sure they were under a spell. She finished her supper and went upstairs. A large suitcase lay open on the bed—how long was she supposed to be away? She added two of her bed toys, her alarm clock and a favorite sweater Mum had left out because it had a hole in one elbow.

"Don't forget my makeup," Demerara said, appearing beside her. "Oh, Lily, I do hope we find Spike! I can't think what's happened to him."

"Has he really not been away before?" Lily asked.

"He's stayed out all night once or twice," Demerara said. "When the rats had one of their vulgar parties— for instance, the time in 1957 when someone dropped a whole crate of gin at Cockfosters station—but nothing like this."

Her voice was oddly muffled. "What've you got in your mouth?" Lily asked.

"Nothing! Nothing at all! Nothing whatsoever!"

Lily thought she looked shifty, but didn't want to offend her. "Do you know where we're going?"

"Not a clue, dear—don't forget the body glitter."

Lily marveled that Demerara could think about body glitter at a time like this, but dropped the tub of glitter into her suitcase. The case was very full, and wouldn't zip up until the stout little cat sat on it.

"Good luck, girls!" a tiny voice called from the wallpaper.

"Good luck with the fur spell!"

"What fur spell?" Lily looked at Demerara. "What are those roses talking about?"

"Nothing—they're just being kind."

"Oh." Lily was suspicious now—but Dad called her before she had time to take it further.

She was glad it was Alan who came to collect them. He was wearing a bulletproof vest and an obvious gun, and it was incredible that Mum and Dad didn't seem to think this was strange. She hugged them both very hard, trying not to wonder when she would see them again.

Caydon was already in the government car. He didn't

look as jaunty as usual; today's drama had rattled him. "My mum thinks I'm going to a camp."

"Mine too."

"And she's treating all the stuff with guns and helicopters like a joke."

"Yes, mine too," said Lily. "As if it happened every day."

"The SMU unit probably released a calming gas, specially aimed at your parents," Alan said, from the front seat. "I had to spray a crowd with it once, when we were towing the dead sea dragon. It stops people from panicking."

Demerara settled herself comfortably in Lily's lap. "Alan, is there any news about Spike?"

"Sorry, I don't know," Alan said. "My orders are to drive you all to the helipad."

"Helipad!" Caydon's face lit up hopefully. "Cool— I've never been in a helicopter!" He grinned at Lily. "You're really scared, I'll bet."

"Shut up," Lily snapped. "This isn't a game—it means something's happened."

"I shouldn't really tell you," Alan said, "it's not in my orders—but there was an explosion on the Piccadilly line."

Caydon wasn't smiling now. "A bomb?"

"Yes, though nobody was hurt—nobody nice, anyway."

Lily said, "You'd tell me if Oz was hurt, wouldn't you?"

"Don't worry." Alan gave her a reassuring smile over his shoulder. "There wasn't a single trace of Oz. They did find one dead body, but that was a member of the gang. I'd better not say any more."

"Oh, I do hope there's some nice food wherever we're going!" Demerara sighed. "Spike catches most of our food and I haven't had a decent meal in days."

"Not long now," Alan said. "The emergency helipad's in Highbury Fields."

This was the large, flat green space at the other end of the Holloway Road, only ten minutes away in the evening traffic. Lily's heart sank at the thought of going in a helicopter, but she was determined not to show this to cocky Caydon.

When they reached Highbury Fields, Alan drove the car right across the grass, to where a helicopter waited noisily, its propellers clattering—a very small, fragile helicopter, as it looked to Lily.

"This is where I hand you over," Alan said. "Good luck."

"Where are we going?"

"It's too dangerous for you to stay on Skittle Street; you're being taken to a safe house."

17

Safe House

Caydon loved every second of the ride in the helicopter. Lily was, at first, rigid with fear—it was like being suspended above the city in a soap bubble. After a few minutes, however, when they hadn't crashed down in flames, she relaxed enough to enjoy the incredible view. London lay beneath them, a vast, glittering carpet of millions of lights. The pilot, a young man named Mike, kindly flew low over the landmarks to give them a good view—the London Eye, the Houses of Parliament, Trafalgar Square and Buckingham Palace.

They flew steadily south, and when it was dark the helicopter landed on a lawn in front of a large house. Lily unstrapped her seat belt and climbed out with Demerara in her arms.

"The sea!" Caydon cried.

The sound of the sea boomed at them through the darkness; the air was keen and salty.

"I hope they have supper laid out," Demerara said. "I'm starving!"

Lily noticed a short, faint fuzz just starting to grow through the holes in the cat's knitted suit. "I think your hair's coming back—I thought Spike said it would take a few weeks."

"Maybe cat fur grows faster than rat fur," Caydon suggested.

Lily looked up at the facade of the house; it was impossible to tell what it looked like in the darkness, with every window blacked out.

A beam of torchlight came bobbing down the lawn toward them; it was the woman known as B62, wearing jeans and a T-shirt instead of her normal smart suit. "Hello, everyone. Sorry to whisk you away like that, but it was a bit of an emergency. Come inside and you'll be brought up to date."

She led them into the house, and they blinked from the sudden bright light. They were in a grand hall, with a fireplace, a large staircase and walls covered with oil paintings and antlers.

"Wow, this is a stately home," Caydon said. "My class went on a visit to a place like this."

B62 smiled. "Welcome to the safe house. I'll show you up to your rooms; the meeting will begin in ten minutes." She started up the stairs.

"Haven't you forgotten something?" Demerara mewed coldly. "Do you seriously expect me to give a full report on an empty stomach?"

"Of course not," B62 said. "We never forget your stomach, Demerara. There'll be a buffet."

"Oh, I do like a buffet." Demerara cheered up. "You can have a little taste of everything."

Caydon was shown into a bedroom on the first floor, while Lily and Demerara were given the room next door; Demerara was especially pleased with the elegant pink cat basket and matching water bowl, and by the time they were back downstairs, she was in a splendid temper.

"J's waiting in the library," B62 said.

On the way to the library they passed an open door and caught a glimpse of a large room with rows and rows of people working at long benches. Some were making fluttering movements with their hands, muttering and producing showers of sparks or puffs of smoke. Others sat very still with their eyes shut; others pored over cards or books of symbols, and there was one very old lady with a crystal ball.

"Whoops, you weren't meant to see that." B62 quickly closed the door. "It's the switchboard, where we send and receive messages of a magical nature, and intercept magical signals."

"Who are those people?" Lily asked.

"You'd probably call them witches; they come from all kinds of backgrounds—we've got everything from a Cambridge professor of physics to a fortune-teller from the Golden Mile at Blackpool." She opened another door. "Here they are, sir."

Lily, Caydon and Demerara walked into a large, grand library, every wall lined with old leather books. The man known as J stood in front of the marble fireplace; just like B62, he was dressed less formally than usual, in a tweed jacket and corduroy trousers.

"My dear young people—and dear old Demerara— well done! Thanks to your quick thinking, a dangerous gang member has been taken out of circulation."

"You mean Janice," Lily said. "Or the woman pretending to be Janice."

"Her real name's Ulrika Klomper," J said. "She's a member of the notorious Schmertz Gang and she's wanted in seventeen countries. I don't have time to explain the gang's ludicrous political demands, but we know the leaders dream of being immortal so that they can take over the world." He frowned. "And we know it's not safe for you at home."

"But what about Mum and Dad?" Lily was alarmed. "Are they safe there?"

"We've posted a twenty-four-hour police guard at both your parents' houses—but we don't think they'll be in any danger. This Klomper woman seems to know that you three have an important connection to the golden molds." He chuckled suddenly. "She was furious about getting caught—she refused to believe me when I told her it was because a talking cat spotted her gun."

"And this is the buffet, is it?" Demerara had turned her attention to a long table beside the window, lavishly covered with bread, cheese, cold meats, salads, chocolate mousses and several kinds of cat food.

"Please help yourself," J said. "I know you've been hungry without Spike to scavenge for you."

"Have you heard from him?" Demerara whipped her head round sharply. "Do you know where he is?"

"Not exactly," J said. "All I can tell you is that I've lent him to the Special Branch—he's managed to infiltrate the gang."

Caydon was impressed. "I didn't think old Spike knew any of them."

"Nothing about that rat would surprise me," Demerara said. "Is he safe? When's he coming back?"

"Let's get ourselves a bite to eat and sit down," J said.

Lily and Caydon looked at each other. This didn't sound like good news—but if J was going to tell them something awful, he'd hardly be loading his plate with slices of chicken potpie. Lily had been too worried to eat much of Mum's lasagne at supper and she was hungry. She took some potpie, and one of the chocolate mousses. Demerara demanded a little bit of every type of cat food, plus slices of smoked salmon and cold chicken, but eventually even she was settled, and J became businesslike.

"Spike was down in the Underground, on his way to the tunnel with the sealing fudge—he was sure this was Isadore's hideout. But some of the gang members had got there first. He stumbled on a couple of them laying explosives."

"But how did they know about it?" Caydon burst out. "They must have someone working inside the SMU."

"That's not possible," J said firmly. "It is possible, however, that they have some kind of magical contact. Spike left a message for Joyce with a passing ghost and followed them—he makes a perfect spy, of course, hidden among all those other rats. And then we lost contact."

"But WHERE is he?" Demerara mewed.

"There was a huge explosion. We had found Isadore's hideout, but it was completely wrecked. You'll be glad to hear that there was no sign of Oz—or Isadore. All we found was one dead gang member, probably from a breakaway faction."

"Is Oz safe?" Lily asked. "Could he have been hurt in the explosion, or—killed?"

J's face was kind. "He's not dead; we searched every crumb of rubble and couldn't find so much as a skin cell. Isadore's taken him somewhere else."

"Do you know where?"

"Not yet—he's been very difficult to pin down. We planted some of our ghost agents around the Albert

Memorial, but they managed to lose him. Now that his hideout has been destroyed, however, he'll be a lot easier to find. We've told the ordinary police to look out for a man and a boy in all the airports and stations. And my best SMU agents are working round the clock to detect the smallest hint of unauthorized magic. As they say in the movies, Isadore can run—but he can't hide."

18

Blue Mountain

O z didn't know how long he had been lying here. His eyes were glued shut and his mouth was like sandpaper. There was a still, damp heat around him, making the air heavy on his skin. Gradually, he became aware of sounds—the whine of a mosquito, birds chattering and shrieking.

He found that he could sit up, and he opened his eyes. "Uncle Isadore?"

He heard the familiar sound of Isadore weeping, and there was a strong smell of drink. They were in a dusty, decaying room with broken wooden shutters and old wallpaper peeling off in long strips. It was furnished with the rickety camp bed Oz was lying on, a crippled chair and a rotting table. Isadore's big suitcase yawned in the middle of the rough wooden floor, spilling out a chaotic heap of clothes, bottles, books and bundles of cash.

The shutter was closed, but light poured through the broken slats—daylight. Oz heaved himself off the bed, threw open the shutter and bathed himself in the glorious light. The sun was hotter here than it was at home, and felt fantastic after all those uncountable days underground. When his eyes adjusted to the dazzle, he gasped aloud.

"Where are we?"

This wooden shack was surrounded by thick, lush green forest. It was a beautiful place, but Oz knew he was a very, very long way from home.

"Uncle Isadore!"

Isadore raised his head from the table. "This is a disaster—I've made a complete mess of everything. Have some rum."

"Is there any water?"

"Tap." Isadore jerked his head toward a cracked sink in one corner.

The water was warm and rusty. Oz drank deeply and splashed his face. His mind was waking up now, and it was all coming back to him—the terrible man with the gun, the explosion.

"Where are we?"

"I had to think quickly," Isadore said. "This is the only one of my houses that nobody knows about. We're in Jamaica."

"Wh-what?"

"The island in the Caribbean."

Oz knew where Jamaica was; he was giddy with shock. "How did we get here?"

"I used a transferring spell my mother invented, which involves harnessing air currents. The force of the explosion actually helped. By the time the smoke had cleared we were halfway across France."

"So there was an explosion; I thought I'd been dreaming."

"Oh, yes, there was an explosion." Isadore started to snivel again. "Thanks to that stupid gang, who can't stop bickering among themselves, my best hideout has been ruined."

Oz's knees were weak; he sat down on the creaking, rusty bed. "What's this place called?"

"We're high up on the Blue Mountain, where they grow the world's most expensive coffee. I tricked this house out of my ex-wife."

"You were married?" Oz was astonished; he couldn't imagine Isadore with a wife.

Isadore wiped his eyes on his sleeve and took another swig of rum. "I came here in the 1970s—partly to get away from certain Nazis who were still after me, and partly to get my hands on a certain very special coffee bean I needed for my magic. It was only grown here— it's all been swallowed by the forest now, but this used to be a farm called Acacia Corner. And it was owned by a young witch who was also very beautiful, so I married her."

"Weren't you still in love with Daisy?"

"Daisy was old by then and thought I'd been dead for years; I was trying to move on. But it didn't work." He shook his head sorrowfully. "Elvira might've been lovely to look at, but she was the bossiest girl on the whole island and she nearly nagged the skin off me."

"Where is she now?"

"She ran away to England—unfortunately, with all the magic coffee berries from her farm hidden in her underwear, so she had the last laugh."

"How long are you planning to stay here?"

"How long?" Isadore let out a bitter little snigger. "I don't know and I don't care. Months—years—as soon as the gang and the government stop hounding me."

"But—" Oz's chest tightened with fear. "I can't wait all that time. I'm starting my new school soon—and I can't miss our baby being born."

"WHY?" Isadore wasn't listening. "WHY does everything I touch turn to ashes?" His head dropped onto the table, and a second later, he was snoring.

Oz frantically tried to organize his thoughts. His great-great-uncle was asleep and the door was open; he could escape, but where to? He went outside, shading his eyes against the sun. The shack was surrounded by thick trees and undergrowth, full of exotic birds and gorgeous flowers. Looking nervously behind him to make sure Isadore wouldn't follow, he ventured through the bushes. Suddenly, a huge and stunning view of a mountainside covered with dense greenery was spread out before him, falling away beneath him for miles and miles without a single house or human in sight.

He turned back to the shack; running away would be stupid when he had no idea where he was going. It would be dark quite soon, and it made him strangely uncomfortable to think about how Isadore would feel if he woke from his drunken stupor to find him gone.

His stomach rumbled; they would need something to eat, and there obviously weren't any shops around here. The overgrown garden outside the shack was filled with huge butterflies that looked quite meaty; maybe he would end up having to hunt them. He rummaged through Isadore's hastily packed suitcase. He had managed to shove in a few bits of food. Oz found half a loaf of sliced white bread and a few tins of baked beans.

There was also a box of matches and Oz spent a long time trying to build a fire. The fireplace inside the shack was choked up with rubbish, so he built his fire on a small patch of cracked concrete outside the door. None of the twigs he found burned properly; he had used up half the matches by the time he coaxed out a flame.

The bread was stale. Oz stuck a slice on the end of a stick and tried toasting it. The bread turned black and hard and tasted of burnt brick, but he used it to scoop cold baked beans out of the tin because he couldn't find a spoon. Though it wasn't the tastiest meal he'd ever eaten, he did feel a lot better afterward. The sun sank and the shadows deepened. The insects dancing under the overhanging acacia branches gradually turned to little specks of fire—fireflies, Oz realized, captivated. Despite being so worried about getting home, he couldn't help enjoying being out in the open, under a sky filled with stars, breathing in delicious scents of flowers and woodsmoke.

"What time is it?" Isadore stumbled out into the darkness, still clutching his bottle of rum.

"I don't know."

"Nobody's come after us, anyway." He sat down on the concrete beside Oz. "You'd be dead by now if they had."

Oz asked, "Who was that man with the gun—the man you killed?"

"I never knew his name. He was my contact among the gang. I have no idea how he found my hideout." Isadore picked up a piece of the burnt bread and nibbled it absently. "I had to kill him; he was going to kill you, and I couldn't bear for you to die."

"Thanks."

"It's polite of you to thank me, dear boy—especially when I've managed to get us into such a mess. What on earth can I do now?"

Oz considered this. "The gang members can't kill you. The worst they can do is lock you up."

"No—that is NOT the worst they can do. If I don't make that immortality chocolate, the gang will tear my entrails out every night at six, like Prometheus chained to the rock."

"Who?"

"He's an immortal chap in Greek mythology. But even that won't be the worst of it. If they don't get the chocolate, they'll kill—you." Isadore's voice was very quiet. "Because they'll know that when I abducted you, I laid myself open to the most appalling pain a human can suffer—the pain of loving someone, and then losing them."

It was alarming to know that Isadore loved him, but impossible not to be moved by his loneliness.

"Uncle Isadore, why don't you just give yourself up? The government won't tear out your entrails." (Or kill anyone, he could have added.)

"I don't fancy being locked up in prison, thank you," Isadore said sharply. "I've committed so many terrible crimes that I'd get a life sentence—think what that would mean. I'd sit there year after year in my suit, and you'd grow old and die—and so would your children and grandchildren. Frankly, there are times when I wish I'd never made myself immortal."

"It can't be much fun," Oz said thoughtfully, "being immortal all by yourself."

"You're a nice boy to try to understand," said Isadore. "But I can't give myself up. It's not going to happen." He shivered. "It gets cold here in the evenings. Let's go inside. You can keep the camp bed and I'll sleep on the floor."

A voice wound through Oz's dreams, high and distant. "Isadore! Isadore! Isadore!"

He woke up, and it was still calling: "Isadore!"

Isadore himself lay on the floor on a heap of clothes, gripping his bottle of rum and snoring.

It was the dead of night, but the tropical moon rode high in the sky and the decayed room looked as if it had been daubed with ghostly white paint. The trees and shrubs whispered and stirred as night creatures scuttled and occasionally shrieked.

"Isadore!"

Oz rolled off the creaking camp bed. The voice was outside. He opened the door and glanced around. There was nobody to be seen.

Maybe I was dreaming, he thought.

"Isadore!" It came again.

Suppose the gang had found him? Oz wished he had a weapon. Diving back into the house, he shook his great-great-uncle's shoulder.

"Uncle Isadore—wake up—there's someone calling you outside!"

"Mmmmm—what?"

"Wake up—there's someone here!"

Isadore sat up, groaning. "What're you talking about? There's nobody here."

"Isadore!"

"Good grief, what was that?" Isadore scrambled to his feet. "Stay behind me, Oz." Holding the rum bottle up in one hand like a club, he crept out into the overgrown garden.

"Isadore!"

"Good grief, it's coming from the rainwater barrel!"

Around the side of the house was a big wooden barrel, green with moss. A greenish light seeped out of it. This was not a gang member.

"Stay close, dear boy!" Isadore clutched his hand. Together, they walked slowly to the barrel and dared to look inside.

The surface of the water was lit like a cinema screen. Oz gasped with the shock of it. In the middle of the magic screen was the round face of an angry black lady with short gray hair. "And about time!" she shouted. "I knew I'd find you there, Isadore Spoffard!"

"Wh-who are you?"

"Who am I? The rightful owner of that farm, for a start!"

In the ghostly half-light, Isadore's face was a mask of horror. "Elvira?"

"YES—you lying, selfish, good-for-nothing SKUNK! I'm your ex-wife—in case it slipped your mind!"

"What do you want?"

"I'm working for the SMU now, you WEASEL. They'll be glad to hear where you are."

"Elvira, please—don't betray me! Don't tell them!"

The plump brown face on the surface of the water was frowning. "As usual, you're only thinking about yourself. I'm here because of this boy—hello, Oz."

"Oh—hello." Oz was startled; he hadn't thought she could see him.

"This boy must go home, Isadore."

"No! I can't be alone again!"

"I've been looking into the future."

"You always were good at that," Isadore said. "It was how you found out I was after your coffee berries."

"I just wish I'd thought of doing that spell earlier," Elvira's face said crossly. "For instance, the day I met you! But this isn't about you. I've seen his future and he must get home IMMEDIATELY."

"What is it?" Oz shivered with apprehension. "What did you see?"

Elvira's face softened. "Perhaps I shouldn't tell you."

Instinctively, Oz gripped Isadore's hand more tightly. "If something bad's going to happen to me, I think I'd rather know about it."

"You're a brave boy," Elvira said. "But I must warn you, it won't be easy."

"I don't care." Oz felt cold and sick, but he knew he had to know the truth.

"I'll show you the picture," said Elvira. "Keep staring at the surface of the water."

As Oz looked, Elvira's face melted into a mist, and another picture began to form.

He saw an aerial view of a green park, with a small red-brick chapel in the middle. As they swooped down closer, he saw that the park was a large cemetery filled with gravestones. Three people were walking slowly toward the chapel—Oz caught his breath as he recognized his parents and Lily.

They were huddled very close together, and all crying. Mum was carrying a tiny white coffin.

"The baby!" Oz choked. "Our new baby!"

He had never seen his mother look so sad; the longing to put his arms around her was so intense that it hurt. And he knew she needed him. He felt a sharp, physical pain that was like his heart breaking.

The terrible picture faded and Oz was left staring at the scummy surface of the water in the barrel.

He heard a great desolate cry ripping out of him, as if it belonged to someone else.

"Oz!" choked Isadore. "My dear boy!"

"Take me home!" Oz shouted. "Take me home NOW—let me go—I HATE YOU—I HATE YOU!"

In all his time as Isadore's prisoner, Oz had never cried. Now the tears burst out of him in a great wave of despairing rage. His hands curled into fists and he began to hit Isadore. He roared and screamed into the empty air until he was exhausted, and then threw himself down on the camp bed and cried himself into oblivion.

19

Sacrifice

The first thing he was aware of was a smell of coffee. Slowly, painfully, Oz returned to consciousness. Before he became fully conscious, the memory of the terrible vision he had seen engulfed him and his sore eyes stung with yet more tears.

He was lying on the camp bed and Isadore was sitting beside him, staring at him intently.

The smell of coffee came from a metal coffeepot in the fireplace; Isadore had cleared it and built a neat fire. He had propped up the sagging table. Oz saw a loaf of bread and a small basket of eggs.

"Good morning," Isadore said. "Please don't hit me again."

Isadore looked different. Oz raised himself on one elbow to look at him properly. His face was pale and haggard, but he had shaved and dressed himself in a respectable white linen suit.

"I'm sober," said Isadore. "For the first time in about sixty years."

"Oh." Oz's head felt thick and woolly, and the misery lay on him like a lead weight.

"Sit up properly and have some toast and coffee. I walked to the nearest farm and bought some decent food."

Oz struggled upright. Isadore gave him a tin mug of sweet, milky coffee and a big slab of toast generously spread with condensed milk. They tasted very good and made Oz feel a lot stronger.

"Would you like some fried eggs?"

"I—I didn't know you could cook eggs."

"I can when I'm sober. The world is a very different place this morning." Isadore spooned a gloopy lump of condensed milk into his coffee. "Before you say one word, Oz, I've made a great decision—I'm taking you home."

"Home!" Oz started crying again. "But what shall I do? I can't tell them what I saw!"

"Hear me out, dear boy; you need to know the whole story. Have some more coffee."

"Actually—yes, please." Oz held out his mug. "I didn't think I liked coffee, but this is fantastic."

"It's Blue Mountain, the greatest coffee in the world. I'm glad you're feeling a bit better."

"I'm sorry about—you know—last night," Oz said. "I don't hate you."

"My dear boy, I deserved it all. And I ought to thank

you; it set me to thinking as I haven't thought in years and years—since I was the man who fell in love with Daisy. After Elvira showed us that ghastly picture of the future, your grief clawed into my mummified old heart. I couldn't bear to see you so sad. As usual, I tried to dull the pain with drink, but I finished the bottle and didn't have any more."

"You drank that whole bottle!"

"I know, I know—enough to kill several people who aren't immortal. I must admit, I went out looking for more rum. But it was a long way to the nearest farm and as I stumbled through the moonlit forest I began to sober up. And at first it was horrible. When I was sober I had to remember the first time I saw that terrible look on someone's face—something I've spent a very long lifetime trying to forget." He let out a sigh.

"What do you mean?"

"Oz, I hope you never know remorse like I suffered last night."

"Remorse?" Oz wasn't sure what he was talking about.

"It was Daisy's face after her husband died—after I killed him."

"So you were sorry after all."

"Yes," Isadore said. "When it was too late. Last night, in the middle of the forest, I thought about Pierre and Marcel. I seemed to see them so clearly—it was as if they walked beside me. My brothers were good men, Oz. I begged them to forgive me, and wished, wished, wished that the past could be changed! And in my agony I found myself thinking about an old Italian novel I read, while I was living in Venice in the 1950s. It was about a bandit who was so incredibly evil that nobody even dared to say his name, and people just called him the Nameless One. He had wealth and power, but his murderous lifestyle had started to disgust him. One day the Nameless One kidnapped a young girl—and her youth and goodness moved him to face up to his past and repent—and then it hit me! Don't you see?"

"See what?" Oz was bewildered; his great-great-uncle was a different man, filled with energy and excitement.

"Last night I was the Nameless One! I had kidnapped a young and innocent person—I'm so sorry, Oz! Your grief last night made me see my wickedness. I found myself longing for a way to make amends—and then I began to think about the awful thing Elvira showed you. And it suddenly came to me—here was a picture I could do something about!"

Oz's heart beat faster. "What do you mean?"

"The past can't be changed—but the future can; the future hasn't happened yet. And then I knew what I had to do."

"Can you change that picture?"

"Not on my own. But when I thought about Pierre

and Marcel, I remembered something from a very long time ago—our mother's special recipe."

"A recipe for chocolate?"

"Not exactly; it had been handed down in her family for hundreds of years. She was a witch."

"I know," Oz said. "Demerara told us. What did her recipe do?"

Isadore's eyes narrowed thoughtfully. "She wouldn't tell us in so many words; she said we'd only be able to make it if we could work it out for ourselves. But I did work it out, because I saw her using it. When we were little boys, our father's best apprentice fell ill. He had a terrible cough and every day he got weaker and weaker, until he couldn't come to work. I think he had something called tuberculosis—a lot of people died of that before antibiotics were invented. But Mother went to see him and took me with her—I can't remember where the other two were—and I saw her give this dying boy a spoonful of something from her handbag. He was back at work a week later, glowing with health. And when I asked Mother about it, she said that in some circumstances, her special family recipe could restore the dying."

"Do you mean—" Oz was making a tremendous effort to understand. "Had she invented antibiotics?"

"No, it was the purest magic, and only worked—so Mother maintained—on those with the purest hearts."

Isadore's dark eyes were clear; he held his cup in hands that no longer trembled. "And nothing on earth is as pure as the heart of a little baby."

"What? What are you saying?"

"I can't make any promises, Oz—this is a very long shot. But if I can find my mother's special recipe—"

"Is it lost?"

"Yes, but if I have the magical resources I know I can find it. You see, it wasn't written down on paper. Just before she died, Mother pressed a silver coin into my hand, whispering, 'You can read it if you're good enough.' It was covered with tiny, tiny writing and I never managed to read it, though I spent every spare moment trying. I lost the coin, but I'm pretty sure one of my brothers stole it. I always suspected Marcel and all his magic stuff was put in the SMU vault."

"It wasn't Marcel," Oz said, suddenly remembering. "It was Pierre—I saw him in the Time-Glass! I saw him take something out of your pocket!"

"Pierre? Are you sure?"

"I couldn't see what he took—but it could've been that, couldn't it?"

Isadore was surprised, and very thoughtful. "Pierre! If Pierre took the coin, it'll be in the secret safe he made at Skittle Street."

"Would you be able to read the tiny writing now?"

"If I have the right backup from the SMU, I can read

the recipe and make Mother's special cordial—and there's a chance that I can save the baby."

Oz's heart gave a great leap of hope that made him breathless. "You can?"

"It's the longest of long shots—I'll need all three golden molds, and any number of magic cacao beans—but I know I can use Mother's recipe to make a new kind of chocolate—the greatest of my career—chocolate that brings real life instead of eternal damnation! I'll do my very best."

Oz burst into tears again, and before he knew what he was doing, he had thrown his arms around Isadore and was sobbing into his bony shoulder. Isadore was surprised, but he hugged Oz hard, and afterward had to wipe his eyes and blow his nose.

"The farmer who sold me the food also sold me an old jeep—at a ridiculous price, but at least he filled it with gas, and we can drive away from here as soon as you're ready."

Oz wiped his face with his T-shirt, feeling ashamed of crying and trying to get his head round the amazing prospect of going home. "What about your mother's spell?"

"Far too dangerous for you—I can see that now that I'm sober. And if possible I'd like to travel on a proper flight, where there's a film and people bring you dinner. I'd better contact the government before we go, or they'll arrest me before I can make my chocolate." Isadore looked gloomy. "Oh crumbs—I'll have to talk to Elvira again!"

They both went outside, to the mossy water barrel; the garden was beautiful in the sparkling early-morning sunlight, and Oz's spirits soared.

Isadore leaned over the barrel, frowning down at the surface of the magic screen. He murmured a few words under his breath. The water misted, and when it cleared, Elvira's face had returned.

"Oh, it's you. Make it quick—I'm at work." She seemed to be bending over a sink.

"Hello, Elvira."

She raised her eyebrows. "Hmm, you don't look so drunk today."

"I'm totally sober," said Isadore. "And for once in my life, I'm taking your advice—I'm bringing Oz straight home."

The stern brown face lifted into a beaming smile, like the sun rising. "Good gracious! You could knock me down with a feather—and that's not so easy these days. What's the catch?"

"There's no catch, I swear—but I do have certain conditions." Isadore launched into a quick version of the story he had told Oz, about the special recipe and the life-giving chocolate he could make with it.

Elvira listened intently, and was silent for a few

moments when he had finished. "How are you going to make the government trust you? They'll think this is a heartless trick to get the molds."

"They MUST trust me," Isadore said. "It's my only chance to make up for my past by changing the future—please, Elvira, help me to make amends!"

"Will you talk about the gang?"

"I'll sing like a canary!"

"Please, Elvira—" Oz blurted out. "Please help him make the chocolate."

The face in the water smiled at him kindly. "Do you think he's tricking us?"

"No—Isadore saved me from the gang members and he's really nice."

Far away, wherever she was working, Elvira laughed. "That makes a change! When I was married to him he was a complete— Oh, all right! For your sake I'll see what I can do. Now I must be off." The picture turned back into water.

"Well," Isadore said, "I'll cook those eggs, and then we'll pack up."

The sober Isadore was a perfectly competent cook. He made an omelette—sprinkling in herbs he picked from the overgrown garden—and it was surprisingly delicious.

Oz helped him to stuff his possessions back into the suitcase. "Hey—you brought the violin!" He was so pleased to see it that he hugged the shabby case. "I thought it had been blown up."

Isadore smiled. "I couldn't bear to leave it behind when you made it sing so beautifully. I think I'll give it to you."

"Really?" Oz felt a spark of actual happiness (something that had been in very short supply since his kidnapping); this violin was better than the one he had at home, and must once have cost a fortune. "What about you—won't you need it?"

"No. Being sober has made me remember that I don't have any talent."

It was a nervous journey for Oz; he longed to get home so desperately that he was afraid something would go wrong. But the new, sober Isadore got them to Kingston Airport and onto the Air Jamaica plane with no trouble at all (though Oz had no idea what he was doing about passports) and they had luxurious seats in business class.

"I may as well enjoy myself while I can," Isadore said. "I'm probably going to spend the rest of eternity in prison."

"It won't be that long," Oz said. "And when you get out, you can come and live with me, if you like." Oddly enough, he meant this; he was sure Isadore's repentance was genuine.

"Thank you, dear boy." Isadore's thin face was almost cheerful.

"Would you like a pillow, sir?" The air stewardess leaned over them and quickly flashed a card with a bar code and a fingerprint. In a whisper, she added, "You'll be met at Heathrow."

To Oz's delight, the policeman waiting for them at passport control was Alan—grinning all over at the sight of Oz.

"Everyone's fine—nothing to worry about—but my orders are to take you to the safe house. Lily and Caydon are there already."

"And my parents are OK?"

"They're great."

"You seem apprehensive, Officer," Isadore said. "Rest assured, I won't give you any trouble."

"Sorry, sir." Alan was so embarrassed that his whole head turned scarlet. "My orders are to put the cuffs on you."

"Handcuffs? Am I a prisoner?"

"Yes."

"Oh, well—I suppose I shouldn't be surprised." Isadore held out one wrist and allowed himself to be handcuffed to Alan.

They were led to a helicopter; Oz couldn't get over

how wonderful the normal damp summer night air felt on his skin. When the helicopter rose into the air, his heart rose with it. Now that he was about to see Lily, he realized how lopsided he had been without her.

"Tell me, Alan," Isadore said, "what are your orders for our arrival?"

"Oz will be allowed to see Lily, and then he has to go to bed. And—well, I have to take you to the cells."

"The cells? But I must see the man known as J!"

"It's one in the morning, sir. He'll see you later."

"Later isn't good enough," Isadore snapped. "I don't care what you have to do, but I must talk to him immediately. Tell him I'm not thinking of my own skin for once—this is for Oz and Lily, and it's a matter of life and death."

20

Home

Lily flung herself at him like a tornado the moment he was through the grand front door.

"OZ! OZ!"

They hugged each other so hard they almost fell over; the happiness was incredible and the other voice fizzed between them like an electrical wire.

"Hey, Oz!" He got a rough hug from Caydon. "You don't look as if you've been tortured."

"How nice to see you, dear," a familiar voice mewed.

"Demerara—what on earth—?" Oz gaped at the extraordinary sight of the immortal cat in her mauve bodysuit.

"Long story!" Lily said hastily. "What happened to evil Isadore?"

"Alan took him to see J," said Oz. "He's not really evil anymore. That's another story." He glanced around at the towering entrance hall, with its oil paintings and impressive staircase. "Where are we?"

"No idea," Caydon said, laughing. "But it's great; there's a private beach. And a canteen full of witches."

"What?"

"It's a center for unexplained communication," Lily said. "They work around the clock in four-hour shifts."

"And you want to watch out for the old bag with the crystal ball," Caydon said. "She can see the future, but never the bits you want to know about—she yelled at me yesterday, and said that when I'm old I'll get a hernia."

"Caydon was skateboarding in the corridor and he crashed into her." Lily stared at Oz. "What's wrong?"

"Nothing."

"You're not happy enough."

"Are Mum and Dad OK?"

"Fine; I spoke to them a couple of hours ago. What's up? I know there's something."

B62 came out into the hall. "Welcome back, Oz. J is still tied up with Isadore and says you should go straight to bed; you're sharing a room and bathroom with Caydon."

"Great." Oz was glad not to be left alone in this house full of witches and soothsayers, and he had missed Caydon's uncomplicated company.

"Lily and Demerara are just next door; they'll take you to breakfast."

Oz was suddenly aware of how tired he was; he had

been too keyed up to sleep on the plane. After the disused tube station and the Jamaican shack, the bedroom he was shown into looked like the pinnacle of luxury. The SMU had even collected his clothes from Skittle Street and his jeans and sneakers looked like old friends. Late as it was, Oz couldn't resist a long, hot shower.

Before they fell asleep, Caydon asked, "Has Isadore really stopped being evil?"

"Yes."

"You believe him?"

"Yes," Oz said. "Yes, I do." He did believe this; and he had faith that the new, reformed Isadore could change that terrible picture of the future. He fell into the most comfortable sleep he'd had since his kidnapping.

They had breakfast the next morning in a big, bright modern canteen with rows of long tables. Though it was still early, the canteen was bustling. Oz, Lily and Caydon queued at the counter with their plastic trays, and Demerara bagged the best table beside the large window, which had a magnificent view of the sea.

Lily brought Demerara a sausage and pulled off the skin for her. While Demerara ate it, she told Oz the story of her burnt fur. As she kept mewing to anyone who would listen, this was her first day without her mauve suit—her portly form was now covered with thick golden-brown fuzz like velvet. "It's pretty, isn't it? And it just appeared overnight—I couldn't tear myself away from the mirror for ages. If I only knew where Spike was, I'd be RADIANT."

"Spike's lost?" Oz said.

"He's away spying on the gang," Lily said. "J said there was an explosion."

They began to exchange their incredible stories. Lily and Caydon told Oz about the enormous cat, the mutant rat and the gang member posing as the new tutor. Oz ate scrambled eggs on toast and told the story of his imprisonment, the Jamaican farm and Isadore's dramatic change of heart. He left out Elvira and the dreadful vision.

"You're leaving something out," Lily said. "Don't bother lying to me." Her voice was not unkind. "I know you too well."

"Caydon, dear." Demerara daintily licked one velvet paw. "Would you fetch me another sausage?"

"Yes, Your Majesty." Caydon jumped up and went back to the counter—accidentally jostling a very old lady in a spangled headscarf. "Sorry."

"You again!" The old lady scowled. "Young man, you watch where you're going—you wouldn't be so saucy if you could see how bald you're going to look at your daughter's graduation!"

"That's Mrs. Fladgate," Lily whispered to Oz. "She

works with a crystal ball; she's the one who told Caydon about his future hernia."

Oz decided to keep well out of Mrs. Fladgate's way; he already knew too much about the future.

After breakfast, B62 told them they could walk in the garden for half an hour. The day was breezy, but clear and bright, and the three of them—and the cat—walked to the edge of the cliff to look at the waves breaking briskly on the small sandy beach below.

"I'm getting cold," Demerara said. "Caydon, dear, pick me up and carry me indoors."

"OK," he said, bending down to scoop her into his arms.

"You don't have to do absolutely everything she tells you," said Lily.

"Oh, I don't mind." Caydon was cheerful. "It's sort of like having a very bossy little sister, or a cuddly toy that answers back."

"Don't be cheeky—cuddly toy indeed!" The immortal cat settled herself comfortably and Caydon carried her back to the house.

Oz and Lily lingered a little way behind him.

"Give me your phone," Oz said. "I want to talk to Mum and Dad."

"What's going on?" asked Lily. "Will I find out what you're not telling me?"

"I don't know." Oz couldn't pretend not to know what she was talking about; she knew his mind as well as he did.

She slipped her hand into his. "It must be something very bad."

"It is."

"I won't pester you," Lily said. She took her phone from her pocket and handed it to Oz. "But I want you to know that you don't have to worry—I won't freak out. I'm a lot braver these days. Even Mum and Dad have noticed. Mum says it was good for me not to rely on you for everything. They think you've been at music camp, by the way. You've had a wonderful time and visited wherever Mozart was born."

"Salzburg," Oz said automatically. "Where do they think we are now?"

"On an outward-bound holiday in the Lake District." She added, "We're loving it."

Oz heard his mother's phone ringing and swallowed the lump that rose to his throat.

"Oz! How wonderful to hear your voice, darling—thanks so much for all the lovely postcards."

"It was great," Oz said. "Are you—are you OK?"

"Me? I'm fine—my bump's getting bigger by the day! It's not due for another three weeks, but the doctor says it might be sooner—Bruce, it's Oz!"

"Fantastic to hear you, Oz," Dad said. "Can't wait to have you back on Skittle Street. It's as quiet as a tomb here, isn't it, Emily?"

Oz didn't trust himself to say any more to his poor parents. He gave the phone back to Lily, who told some amazing lies about what they were supposedly doing in the Lake District.

"Got to go now—we're off rappelling. Love you!" She switched off her phone. "It's something to do with them, isn't it? Don't worry, I won't keep asking."

He was grateful for this, and a bit surprised; Lily really did seem to have got braver. "I'll tell you the important bit—Isadore must be allowed to make his special chocolate."

"I can't think why you like that man," Lily said. "You should hear what he did to Demerara."

"He's changed."

The man known as J was waiting for them in the library. Isadore stood beside the empty fireplace drinking a cup of coffee. Oz was glad to see that he was no longer in handcuffs.

"Good morning, dear boy—J and I have finally thrashed out a deal."

"I don't much like it," J said. "I'm trusting you because I don't have a choice."

"FIEND!" shrieked Demerara. She launched herself at Isadore like a velvet missile, digging her claws into his shoulders. "MURDERER! KIDNAPPER! CAT DROWNER! RAT BURNER!"

It took both Caydon and Lily to pry the furious, spitting cat off him.

"Ouch," Isadore said. "Good grief, it's Pierre's cat! I left you in a bucket of water, didn't I? Sorry I had to do that."

"SORRY!"

"I advise you to let bygones be bygones," Isadore said. "I'm working for the good guys now."

"I wouldn't trust you an INCH!"

"Demerara!" J said sternly. "Calm down and behave like a secret agent—or I'll put you outside!"

"But I've been waiting to claw him to shreds since 1938!"

"You'll have to wait a little longer."

"Pooh!" Demerara flopped sulkily into Lily's lap.

"Now kindly shut up." J was not in a good mood. Oz could see that he didn't like being forced to trust Isadore. "Welcome back, Oz—it's a great relief to see you."

"You will let him make the chocolate, won't you?" Oz asked.

J's face showed that he knew about Elvira's vision of the future. "Yes—as soon as I get confirmation that he's telling the truth about the gang."

"He told me their target was the Albert Hall."

"I need more than that, I'm afraid; he might have made it up."

Isadore finished his cup of coffee. "My dear J, you behave as if we had all the time in the world!"

There was a knock at the door and B62 came in with a large padded envelope. "Excuse me, sir; this just came for you."

J took the package. He opened one end, and a voice floated out: "Morning, all!"

"Spike!" gasped Demerara. "But—what's happened to you?"

"I got run over, and I haven't popped back into shape yet—somebody help me out!"

J put his hand inside the padded envelope and pulled out what looked like a furry pancake. Spike was squashed flat, with a tire print down his back. His head was the only part of him that moved. Lily was so pleased to see him that she nearly kissed his greasy little head. Caydon ruffled his fur affectionately.

"Oz—nice to see you, mate!"

"Nice to see you, Spike—are you really OK?"

Spike managed to turn his head toward Isadore. His whiskers bristled. "What's HE doing here?"

"He's changed sides," Demerara mewed crossly. "Which means we're not allowed to claw him to shreds."

"You've been spying on the gang members, Spike," J said.

"Yessir. I can't tell you where they are because I lost them on the M11 when I got thrown out of a car window and run over by a truck. But I did learn that their target was the Albert Hall—until they had to cancel it because one of them got killed, and he'd had some sort of quarrel with the others—they couldn't stop falling out! I got squashed before I could find out where they planned to bomb next."

J looked at Isadore. "So you were telling the truth."

"I don't blame you for being suspicious," Isadore said. "I'd be the first to admit that my history up to now has been one long list of misdeeds."

"Those gang members don't like you," Spike said. "You double-crossed them, and when they find you they're planning to tear out your entrails every night at—"

"Thank you, I know what they're planning." Isadore looked at J. "We'll need protection."

"You'll get it," J said in a kinder voice. "You'll get everything you need."

21

Dr. Sneed

"Our last tutor turned out to be a spy," Mum said. "That was probably why she had nothing to say about her teaching methods."

"I am not a spy," the new tutor said. "As for my methods, I once had great success with a dyslexic girl who worked in a business of mine. Instead of rubbing in her weaknesses, I concentrated on her strengths. Her math was poor, but she learned to manage money better than the chancellor of the exchequer—and what else is math for?" He smiled at the twins as they came into the kitchen. "You must be Oz and Lily."

"Hi, kids," Mum said cheerfully. "This is Dr. Ian Sneed. He's going to be Lily's tutor, and he's also giving some lessons to Oz."

Under the table, Demerara let out a snarl. "Just tell me when you want me to SCRATCH him."

Lily edged closer to Oz. He was pleased to find Isadore lounging in their kitchen as if he owned the place, but she was still scared of him.

"Well, I'll pop out now, if that's OK." As usual, Mum had totally swallowed the SMU cover story. "See you later."

The moment the front door slammed behind her, Isadore said, "Goodness, your parents are easy to bamboozle—OW! Oz, will you kindly stop this cat from scratching me?"

"Sorry," Demerara said sulkily. "The temptation is just so hard to resist." She trotted out from under the table.

"Your fur's grown again," Oz said.

Lily ran her hand across the cat's golden back. The velvet fur was longer and softer now. "Mmm, this feels lovely—I didn't think it would grow back this fast."

For a fraction of a second, the square emerald eyes were shifty. "Neither did I."

"It looks a bit different," Lily said, bending down to examine it. "I swear there's a slight curl."

"Oh—fancy that!"

"Lily," Isadore said, "I haven't introduced myself to you properly. Please try not to be afraid of me—your brother will tell you I'm here to help."

"He is," Oz assured her. "It's really important that you trust him."

"This is about the secret thing, isn't it?" Lily looked from Oz to Isadore; they were creepily easy in each other's company.

"Yes—I can't say what it is, but he's our only hope. You have to trust him."

"And so do you," Isadore told Demerara. "You and the rat are a vital part of this operation. Where is he?"

"Spike's having a smoke in the next door's gutter," Demerara said. "I expect he'll be along in a minute. Why do you want us?"

"I need to get into Pierre's safe."

"Certainly NOT! I don't care how long you leave me in a bucket of water this time—I'm NEVER going to tell you how to get in—so THERE!" If cats could stamp their feet, Demerara would have stamped hers.

"But you must!" Oz was alarmed; Lily could feel his gnawing anxiety.

"I made a solemn promise to Pierre, the very day before he died." The green eyes shot poison at Isadore. "I can see him now. He sat me on his knee and said, 'Demerara, I think my evil brother Isadore is trying to kill me—don't ever let him near my magic safe!' I promised him, and I've kept that promise ever since."

"For pity's sake," Isadore snapped. "Someone tell this idiotic animal to cooperate!"

"Please, Demerara." Oz was pale and looked as if he was trying not to cry. "I saw something horrible from the future—it's no use asking what because I won't say—but Isadore is the only person in the world who can change it—if anyone can—please, Demerara!"

Lily knew then why Oz had to trust their wicked great-great-uncle. He didn't need to tell her what horrible thing he had seen. She felt his desolation. Once she would have burst into tears—but this was obviously a very serious emergency, and she needed to keep her head.

She stroked Demerara. "Pierre would be proud of you, but he'd expect you to tell us now. Isadore's given up being wicked to help us."

"Well—he'd better show me some respect."

"I'll grovel as much as you like," Isadore said. "But I don't have time now. Let's assess the damage in the workshop."

It was strange to see Isadore's familiarity with their house. He drained his tea and bustled off to the workshop. "Good grief!"

Oz hadn't been into the workshop since the fire, and he drew in his breath—it was a blackened, ruined mess.

"This was your fault," Demerara told Isadore coldly. "Your postcard did this. I hope you're satisfied."

Isadore took a notebook and pencil from the breast pocket of his linen jacket and began to write busily, muttering to himself. "New separator—new blending paddles—new silver funnels—new roasting pan—dear me, we'll need to start from scratch! We'd better begin with some basic cleaning."

He swept Oz and Lily out to the hardware shop next to

the supermarket and bought mops, scrubbing brushes, buckets, brooms and heavy-duty cleaner, until they were both laden with bags of cleaning stuff.

Caydon was on the pavement outside, with a flat Spike drooping over one shoulder. "What's going on? You look like two Father Christmases bringing really boring presents."

"Ah, the third witch." Isadore handed him a stiff brush. "Just in time to clean out the fireplace."

This was not how Lily, Oz and Caydon had expected to spend their first morning with the evil genius. Isadore gave them all rubber gloves and aprons and set them to work. Caydon scrubbed the fireplace; Oz started sweeping up all the charred rubble on the floor. Lily was told to wash the chocolate stone in the middle of the room in a mixture of warm water and dishwashing liquid. Isadore stood beside her, washing blackened tools in a bowl of hot, soapy water.

"And Demerara, I think the chimney's choked up with soot—would you just run up and down it to clear it? You'll make an excellent flue brush."

"WHAT?" Her silky new fur bristled with outrage. "How DARE you call me a BRUSH?"

"I'll do it," Spike said quickly. "I don't mind a bit of soot."

"Did you hear him, Spike? He thinks I'm a brush! He thinks he can shove me up the chimney!"

"Calm down, old girl!" The rat was still flat, but moving nimbly again. Oz helped him into the chimney and he whisked up it in a thick cloud of soot.

"Well, you don't need me here," Demerara said. "And I mustn't get soot on my fur—"

Isadore stepped in front of her. "Haven't you forgotten something?"

"I don't know what you mean."

"Open the safe!"

"Oh, all right!" Demerara mumbled something and screwed up her eyes. In the blackened wall, the secret door appeared.

"I'm impressed," Isadore said. "I never suspected Pierre was clever enough to come up with something like this." He dropped to his knees and crawled into Demerara's flat. "I'm inside!" they heard his voice calling excitedly. "It's a bit of a mess—I can see Mother's notebooks—OH DEAR HEAVEN! WHAT AM I KNEELING IN?"

Spike flopped out of the chimney like a sooty pancake. "Whoops, he's found my bag of old sheep's liver."

"OH, THAT IS THE MOST UNSPEAKABLY DISGUSTING—" Isadore scrambled out the door, smeared with dirt and white as a sheet. He dived over to his bucket of water and plunged his hands into it, shuddering. "I'm not going in there again!"

"Who invited you?" Demerara was smirking, and

looked so smug that Lily had to stop herself from giggling.

"Sorry about that, Mr. Isadore," Spike said. "Tell you what—I'll go in and clear out all my rotting stuff."

"Thank you, Spike. You're disgusting, but you always were an obliging rodent."

"Now then, you silly old bag," Spike said to Demerara. "Get off your high horse. You know as well as I do—if J says Mr. Isadore's OK now, he's OK."

"But it's so hard, when I've detested him since at least 1935! And I can't bear him trampling all over our cozy little flat."

"Well, if you come and help, he won't have to, will he?"

"I suppose not." Holding her head up proudly, Demerara followed Spike through the little door.

"She's awfully rude to Spike," Lily said, "but she's lost without him."

Isadore dropped another tool into his bucket, looking at Lily thoughtfully. "You're very much like your great-great-grandmother."

"Really?" It was a little embarrassing to know that she looked like the girl Isadore had loved in vain.

"She was the girl I described to your parents."

"The one who had dyslexia?" This was interesting.

"Yes, it often runs in families. And it's often a sign of certain magical abilities."

"Was Daisy magic, then?"

"She wasn't a witch, as our mother was," Isadore said. "But she was tremendously receptive to the unseen—as you and Oz and Caydon are. You especially."

"I'm the most magical! I'm not boasting," she added. "I'm not used to being best at things."

"Daisy had the same low opinion of her own powers," Isadore said. "She started in the business as a kitchen maid, but Mother soon spotted her talents—her brilliant memory, for one thing. Mother predicted we'd all fall in love with her."

"Pierre as well?"

"Oh, Pierre adored her," Isadore said. "Though I suspect he was actually fonder of that ridiculous talking cat."

"Which one of you did your mother want her to marry?" Lily was fascinated; how romantic to have triplets in love with you.

"Mother didn't mind." Isadore carefully dried the silver blade of a knife. "But when Daisy got engaged to Marcel, she wanted to be sure she'd made the right choice. Mother had the same disconcerting gift as my ex-wife—she could conjure pictures of the future. First, she showed Daisy how her life would look if she married Pierre. She saw them both sitting in big armchairs, surrounded by cats, eating cake. They were both very fat. Then she showed Daisy how her life would be if she married me—incredibly rich, with a Rolls-Royce and a yacht—that's what we could have done as a team! Finally, she showed Daisy her life with Marcel—in a boring little house, with a baby. And that was the life she wanted! I ask you!"

"She loved him," Lily said.

"I suppose she did—and to any normal person, that explains everything." Isadore sighed and shook his head. "I think I'm beginning to understand."

The next morning, some builders arrived.

"It's awfully nice," Dad told the twins cheerfully. "Something called the Chocolate Heritage Society has offered to restore the workshop for nothing! We're not using it for anything else; I thought it would be interesting to bring it back to its former glory."

Oz and Lily knew perfectly well that there was no such thing as the Chocolate Heritage Society, even before one of the builders quickly showed his SMU card—the government of magic had given their parents a really amazing talent for not noticing things. These builders worked very fast. While Mum brought them cups of tea, they cleaned and painted and plastered furiously. A shining new metal tank appeared. There were new racks for the tools, new shelves for the molds. By the time Isadore appeared for his next tutoring session, only three days later, the workshop was gleaming and immaculate.

He gazed round it, running his hands over the surfaces. "I can hardly believe it—it's like turning the clock back to the 1930s! I can practically hear the trams on Holloway Road!"

"It's lovely, isn't it?" Mum came in suddenly, making Isadore jump. "I thought Oz and Lily would want to show you; we're all thrilled with it."

"Good morning, Mrs. Spoffard." Isadore had recovered. "I think I'll teach in here this morning."

"Well, the kids will tell you what all this stuff is for," Mum said. "They've been looking up chocolate making on the Internet."

"Fascinating! I can't wait to hear about it."

"I'll bring you a cup of tea—I'm the size of a hippo, but I can still waddle about." She left the room.

"This is most satisfactory," Isadore said. "It has been finished to a very high standard. We'll spend today's lesson making an inventory of the various things inside Pierre's safe—where's that cat?"

"I haven't seen her since yesterday," Lily said.

"WOW!" Spike's head popped out of a saucepan. "Am I in the right place? This is just like the old days!"

"Hi, Spike." Oz scooped him up with one hand; unlike Lily, he wasn't at all squeamish about handling the whiskery little rodent. "How's it going?"

"I've moved all the rotting things," Spike said. "It was hard work shifting it all by myself. The old girl wanted to help—but she was too worried about her new fur."

"This workshop is SPLENDID!" mewed Demerara's voice. "I absolutely LOVE it!"

She strolled into the middle of the floor.

"What's happened to you?" Lily gasped.

"What do you mean, dear?"

"Your fur—it's gone all . . . curly!"

Demerara's golden brown fur was a mass of thick curls, of a kind no cat has ever been seen with.

"Yes, it has grown back with a tiny curl to it."

Oz and Lily started laughing; she was such a bad liar, and the big curls looked hilarious.

"Hmmm." Isadore frowned down at her suspiciously. "I think this cat has been messing about with the magic chocolate again."

"Old girl," Spike said, "you're a dazzler!"

"Thank you, Spike." The curly cat was dignified. "It's completely natural; I have NOT been messing about!"

Mum came back into the room with a tray of tea for Isadore and juice for Oz and Lily. "Here you are, Dr. Sneed; if you need anything else, I'll be upstairs ordering stuff online for the baby."

"Right," Isadore said briskly, when she had gone again, "we're ready to empty the safe and we'll need every pair of hands—Oz, you'd better fetch Caydon."

As soon as they were all assembled, Isadore set them to work. The boys went into the flat with Demerara and began passing out all the magical objects Pierre had hidden there—books, glass jars, boxes and bottles. Lily wiped each object with a duster and handed it to Isadore, who wrote it down in his notebook. Spike and Demerara were supposed to be pointing out the things that were magic, though Demerara spent most of the time giving orders and making objections.

Her cross voice floated out into the workshop. "Mind my cushion! Careful with that saucer! Spike—don't forget the beans I hid under those dead mice!"

Everything that came out was grimy and damp smelling—except Pierre's golden mold.

Oz passed it out the door to Lily, who held it up, fascinated by the beautiful detail of the smiling face.

Isadore let out a long sigh, like air escaping from a balloon. "At last!" His thin face quivered with emotion. He reached out his hand. "AARRRGGH!"

He was hurled across the room and landed in an ungainly heap beside the door. Lily ran over to help him to his feet.

"Good grief," he gasped. "That hurt like Hades! Keep that thing away from me—it nearly burnt my hand off!"

"I can't feel anything," Lily said. "It's just warm, like bathwater."

Isadore leaned against the chocolate stone, blowing

229

on his hand. "My brothers' molds won't have anything to do with me; I suppose because I murdered them. Our mother must have known something about the future. She had these golden molds made for our twenty-first birthday. Pierre got the sun, symbol of life. Marcel got a star, the symbol of love. And she gave me this moon—" he pulled the black velvet bag out of his pocket— "symbol of death."

"Weren't you annoyed?" Lily asked. "I'd have found it a bit insulting."

"It doesn't have to mean death in the right hands," Isadore said. "But mine were the wrong hands. Kindly wrap Pierre's sun in a clean tea towel and take charge of it, so I won't have to touch it again."

When everything had been cleared out of Demerara's flat, Oz and Caydon crawled out (very dusty and cobwebby) to look at the strange collection Isadore had neatly arranged on the stone. There were two mildewed notebooks with rotting leather covers, and an assortment of small glass jars filled with shriveled brown beans.

It didn't look like much, but Isadore was pleased. "I must say it was smart of Pierre to stash these things away—he knew exactly what I'd be after." He picked up one of the jars, with a wistful smile. "That's Mother's writing on the label; she used these beans to make a wonderful truffle called Chocastaire that improved people's dancing—unfortunately we had to take it off the market when a famous dancer called Fred Astaire threatened to sue. But where's the silver coin?"

"What coin?" Demerara asked. "We never had any coins—did we, Spike?"

"Hmm, that could be awkward." Isadore frowned thoughtfully. "I might have to ask J to put his Time-Glass engineers on that one; but it would take time to comb through the past and pinpoint what happened to it. Maybe Pierre was smart enough to put it in the SMU vault for safekeeping—I've tried every spell in the book to get into that vault."

"Pierre had a brilliant mind," Demerara said, "as well as a brilliant heart—didn't he, Spike?"

"Mr. Pierre was an angel," Spike said solemnly. "An angel with a mustache."

A green frown glinted in the cat's curly golden face. "I'm still wondering if I should have opened the safe. He must be spinning in his grave!"

"His grave's in Highgate Cemetery," Spike said. "We nip up there every once in a while, to keep it tidy."

Lily thought how odd it would be to see a grave being tended to by a cat and a rat.

"I remember the funeral as if it were yesterday." Demerara sighed. "It was a triple funeral—even though they only found two bodies—and it was a very grand occasion. The German ambassador was there, the entire

Soviet Union Women's Shot-Putting team and any amount of opera stars—all lovers of great chocolate, mourning the world's greatest chocolatiers."

"Were you there?" Caydon asked Isadore. "I wouldn't like going to my own funeral, but I wouldn't be able to keep away either."

"That is a very cheeky question," Isadore said shortly.

"Of course he went to the funeral," hissed Demerara. "We saw him—didn't we, Spike?"

"He was disguised as a woman," Spike said, "but we spotted him all right. We'd already suspected he wasn't dead."

Isadore was pale. "You don't need to remind me. I'm not the same man—I'm making this chocolate to atone for my crimes."

"Hmm," Demerara said. "I'll believe it when I see it."

"The most important thing is Marcel's mold. I won't be able to touch it—you three must come with me to collect it." Isadore made a few notes, and suddenly gave the extravagantly curly cat a searching look. "And I'll have that Wavio bean you're hiding in your cheek."

"I—don't know what you're talking about!"

"Yes you do—and I refuse to work with someone who looks like a feline Shirley Temple."

"Pooh," said Demerara. Very slowly and sulkily she spat out a small, withered brown bean. "You're so selfish—why shouldn't I have lovely curls?"

Isadore picked the bean up off the floor with a pair of tweezers and dropped it into a plastic bag. "Do you want curly teeth? Curly bones? That's what would have happened if you'd kept that magic cacao bean in your mouth, you ludicrous animal. Kindly stop messing about with things you don't understand. I'm in charge now, whether you like it or not."

22

Reunion

"I came here with my class in Year Five," Caydon said. "I sat on my carton of apple juice and my packed lunch was soaked."

"We came here in Year Four," said Oz.

"And my classwork was the best for once," Lily added. "I drew a picture of one of the ravens. He wouldn't stop staring at me and he wouldn't go away, so I just drew him."

The SMU's secret vault was in the Tower of London. It was a bright summer's day and the ancient gray castle swarmed with tourists. The famous ravens, with their clipped wings, flopped across the smooth lawns. The even more famous Beefeaters posed for photos in their red and gold uniforms. A long line had formed to see the Crown Jewels.

Isadore said something to one of the Beefeaters and they were waved through the main entrance. He led them through a stone arch to the square lawn on Tower Green. Bright blue doors were set into the ancient walls. There was a sentry in a red coat and bearskin, like a toy soldier or a picture on a London tea towel. Two ravens, large and black and angry looking, hopped determinedly after them.

"Those birds are following us," Caydon said.

Isadore was pale and nervous, and kept poring over his notes. "It's because of Lily."

"Me? Why—do I smell of bird food or something?"

"These birds are masterful detectors of magic; when my mother came here they wouldn't leave her alone. Ignore them. This is Devereux Tower, where the SMU has its office."

"Well, this place has got to be extremely haunted," Oz said. "So many people were murdered here. They used to put their heads on the gate."

"The Tower is the most haunted place in London—more than Tyburn, where they burned those Catholics, or Smithfield, where they burned those Protestants." Isadore knocked loudly on one of the blue doors. "But I'm not here to give you a guided tour; this is business."

The door was opened by a straight-backed old man in army uniform. "Isadore Spoffard? Come in quickly, please—and you two clear off."

The ravens, who had been flapping uncomfortably close to Lily's heels, instantly turned round and hopped away.

"Ravens at the Tower are members of the British

Army," the old man said. "They have to obey orders."
He shut the door behind them. "I'm Colonel Turnbull—
officially retired, and unofficially in charge of SMU
business at the Tower."

"These are the children," said Isadore.

"Lily, Oscar and Caydon." The colonel smiled kindly
at them under his white mustache. "Thanks for helping
out. Would you all follow me, please?"

Lily had expected the inside of the building to look
historical, like the rooms they had seen on the school
trip, and was a bit disappointed to be walking along a
functional white-painted corridor that could have been
anywhere. They walked up some stone stairs.

"My back's tingling again," Caydon said. "It feels like
someone's dripping freezing water down my spine."

"Mine too," said Oz. "Uncle Isadore—are you OK?"

Isadore's face was like wax. "I'm feeling a little faint."

"Sorry about that," Colonel Turnbull said. "We've just
done another spraying of anti-ghost paint; my magic
operatives tell me it can sometimes make them ill."

"Aren't you magic?" Caydon asked.

"No, I'm just an ordinary nonmagic person who
can see ghosts. All the buildings here are incredibly
haunted. And not merely with human ghosts—before
the Regent's Park Zoo was built, all kinds of wild animals were kept here."

The colonel stopped in front of a heavy metal door

with a keypad on the wall beside it. He tapped in a long number and the door swung open to reveal a large office with a cheerful view over Tower Green.

The man known as J stood in front of a fireplace that contained a safe. "Good afternoon."

"I see that you don't trust me yet." Isadore collapsed into a chair, mopping his forehead with a handkerchief. "You're as bad as that wretched cat."

"You know perfectly well I'm the only person with the authority to hand over the items in this safe," said J. "You've brought the other molds?"

"Yes. I have my moon. Lily's carrying Pierre's sun." Isadore pulled the black velvet bag containing his mold from his pocket.

Lily took Pierre's mold, wrapped in a freezer bag, from the pocket of her fleece.

J took the two molds, unwrapped them carefully and placed them side by side on the empty desk.

Lily gasped aloud—her spine was fizzing like champagne and the other voice made her and Oz reach for each other's hands.

"It's a bit cold in here," said Caydon.

"A bit? It's deathly!" Isadore leaned back in his chair. "This isn't the anti-ghost paint. It's because the molds are so close to each other; it creates a force field that is particularly agonizing for anyone with a guilty conscience. Let's get this over with!"

"Very well." J punched a series of numbers into the keypad on the safe. He opened it and took out a flat tin case like one of Lily's boxes of watercolor paints, filled with neat squares of different types of chocolate, each one neatly labeled. J placed this on the desk. After this he took out the golden mold they had pulled out of the river: Marcel's star, which caught a shaft of sunlight and blazed gloriously in his hand.

"Unwrap them," Isadore whispered. "Place them close together in a little circle, so that they're touching each other. And the children must stand one behind each mold to complete the circle." He was incredibly pale.

J did as he said. The three golden molds stood together on the desk, and goose pimples rose all over Lily's skin. She and Oz and Caydon stepped behind them.

There was a clap of thunder; the day darkened. The room filled with shadows.

A humming sound came from the three molds, gradually getting stronger and stronger until they almost danced on the polished surface of the table.

More thunder boomed above them; flashes of lightning slashed through the sudden gloom. Lily caught her breath—two figures stood on either side of Isadore's chair. She saw glimpses of them in the lightning: two men with dark hair and mustaches, one stout and one thin.

"NO!" screamed Isadore.

There was a final, shattering clap of thunder—and the weather suddenly changed back to breezy sunshine.

Isadore's chair was empty.

Caydon fainted.

"You can stop teasing me about throwing up now," Lily said. "At least I didn't faint."

"OK, OK," Caydon said crossly. "But I bet you were shocked—those ghosts—and then he wasn't there anymore."

"The ghosts were Marcel and Pierre," said Lily. "I know Pierre from the picture in my bedroom."

"Where did they go, anyway? Does this mean Isadore's dead?"

"I don't think so," Oz said. "He's still immortal. He has to come back." He didn't like to admit how worried he was; if Isadore didn't come back, how could they save the baby?

Colonel Turnbull had opened the window and given them all glasses of iced Coke.

"You mustn't be ashamed of fainting," he told Caydon. "I fainted once, and I didn't have the excuse of being as young as you are."

Caydon looked a little less cross. "What did you see? Was it something here?"

"I saw the bear," the colonel said with a shudder. "Everyone faints when they see the bear."

"Not all animal ghosts are like Edwin," J said. "Many are terrifying enough to make a strong man die of fright. The bear is the ghost of a polar bear that lived here in the Tower in the thirteenth century. He belonged to King Henry the Third. The local people used to enjoy watching him when he went salmon fishing in the Thames; it wasn't full of old trams in those days."

"I'll never forget the night I met him," Colonel Turnbull said. "I'd been to dinner with a friend who was quartered here, and I was enjoying the crisp spring evening on the Green—and suddenly an immense polar bear with snarling, bloody jaws and blazing eyes was bounding across the grass toward me—so real that I could feel its breath on my face in the second before it swiped me with its claws. That was when I fainted."

"Wow." Oz tried to imagine this. "I'm not surprised!"

"Please keep that bear away from us," Caydon said. "I'm not as magical as the others and it would probably kill me."

"I'd love to see it," Lily said; being the brave one was a novelty and she couldn't help swaggering a bit.

"Caydon, you really must get over this notion that you're not as magical as the twins," J said. "Your inheritance is every bit as strong."

"But they've got magic in the family. My family isn't

magical at all. My parents are both bus drivers and my gran's a midwife."

"You'll find a witch somewhere in your ancestry," J said. "People were ashamed of their magic in the old days and tried to cover it up." He glanced at his watch. "Isadore's been gone for over an hour."

"Do you know where he is?" Oz asked anxiously. "He will come back, won't he? He must!"

"He'll be back," said J. "I've seen this kind of switch before. Colonel, could they do something educational while they're waiting?"

"Certainly," Colonel Turnbull said cheerfully. "We'll get an ice cream and watch the ravens having their afternoon tea—the Ravenmaster is a particular mate of mine."

It was good to be out in the afternoon sunlight, licking ice cream and weaving among the hundreds of tourists. Lily loved watching the ravens; her face lit up and her hair crackled joyfully as she fed an angry old bird squares of cheese and hard-boiled egg. Oz would have enjoyed it too, if he hadn't been so worried about Isadore.

To his huge relief, Isadore was in the office when they returned. He was soaking wet, wrapped in a tartan blanket, sipping hot tea.

"Are you OK?" Oz asked. "What happened?"

"I can't tell you in any detail," Isadore said, "but I

saw my brothers and we talked. They have now decided to help us."

"I knew that was Marcel and Pierre," said Lily. "I thought they hated you. Why are they suddenly on your side?"

"Please—I can't say any more." Isadore was white to his lips. "We talked, that's all. Now kindly take us back to Skittle Street."

23

The Boys in the Orchard

"What awful bad luck to fall into the Thames on your educational trip to the Tower," Dad said. "If you're really sure about staying this evening, you must let me lend you some dry clothes."

"Thank you," said Isadore. "It would be a little inconvenient to have to go home in between."

Oz wondered where Isadore was living now that his hideout had been destroyed, and he asked him as soon as they were alone together.

"The department gave me a small room in Regent's Park barracks," Isadore said. "It's a bit of a comedown, but I won't be there for long."

"What do you mean? Are you leaving?"

"My dear Oz, I do believe you really would miss me! But I'm not leaving just yet; there's far too much to do."

The two of them sat at the kitchen table with the back door open, drinking mugs of tea. Isadore looked strange in Dad's old jeans and shirt. He was officially "babysitting" while Mum and Dad were out at the cinema—there was a film Mum particularly wanted to see while she had the chance, before the new baby arrived. Lily was watching television in the sitting room upstairs, with Demerara and Spike.

Oz said, "Nobody else is here. You can tell me what happened today. You know you can trust me not to tell anyone else—not even Lily."

"Yes, dear boy, I do know. Perhaps it will help me to talk about it—my head's still spinning." Isadore sighed and stared out at the weedy back garden, so ordinary and peaceful in the sunset.

The silence stretched on. Oz decided to help him. "Where did you go when your brothers came for you?"

"I was very scared," Isadore said thoughtfully, "because I felt so guilty. But they hadn't come to punish me. Everything went black and the next thing I knew, I was a boy again—a boy of about your age. Pierre and Marcel were with me. We were in the old orchard of our grandfather's house in the French countryside where we spent every summer. And I remembered how it felt to be happy. I remembered how beautiful life was, before I turned wicked and we were the Perfect Three. That's what Mother used to call us. The Perfect Three, working and playing together in perfect harmony!"

"Before you met Daisy," Oz suggested.

"I think it started before then." Isadore was sad. "I floated out of my boyhood body and stood with Pierre and Marcel, watching the children we used to be. And I was already taking more than my fair share of the sweets we were supposed to divide equally. I already thought I was the best and the cleverest. So it's no use blaming Daisy."

"What did they say to you?"

"Nothing much; at first they just wanted me to watch. In fact, whenever I tried to say anything, one of them would say 'Not now—just watch.' So I watched. My dear Oz, I can't describe the agony of seeing those happy boys in the orchard, with their clean consciences and their hopeful hearts! I felt I would have given anything to go back. But that wasn't the purpose of this trip down Memory Lane. Marcel and Pierre made me relive various scenes of my life—which I'd rather not describe—ending with a grand finale in the tram. It was appalling!"

"Did you have to watch the crash again?"

Isadore groaned softly. "Much worse—I had to do the murders again. I was back inside my own former body, and the horror was that I didn't want to commit this crime, but I was unable to stop. I had to crash the tram again, kill all those innocent people and watch my poor brothers drown."

"And that was when you came back?"

"Not quite." Isadore flicked Oz a furtive look. "As I told J, we finally had a chance to talk."

"Where? At the bottom of the river?"

"I don't know where we were—a place where there was just us, the Perfect Three—not so perfect anymore! I knelt and wept and begged them to forgive me."

"And?"

"They both laughed. Marcel told me not to make a song and dance about it. Pierre said I always loved to dramatize. I made an effort to brace up, and then— then—" Isadore frowned, as if trying to remember. "I think we drank some hot chocolate—and we got down to the nitty-gritty."

"What was that?"

"Hmmm?" Isadore had the furtive look again. "You don't need to know the details. We came to an understanding." He fell into silence.

Oz waited to hear more.

"It turns out," Isadore said quietly, "that I no longer want what I thought I wanted."

"You mean, going back in time and making Daisy fall in love with you?"

"I've been offered a chance—a tiny chance—to get something much better."

"Sorry?" Oz was confused.

"You'll understand one day. Shall we have some more tea?" Isadore jumped up, so fast that he had to grab Dad's trousers to stop them from falling down. "We have all the ingredients, Oz. We have the molds, and the blessing of my two brothers—which reminds me, I need to talk to that cat." He hurried upstairs to the sitting room, where Lily, Spike and Demerara were watching TV. "Demerara, give me the silver coin!"

The immortal cat was still annoyed about losing her curls. "For the last time, I don't know what you're talking about."

"Pierre gave you our mother's silver coin."

"He did not!"

"I've just seen him," said Isadore. "He told me—he nicked it from my pocket and gave it to his cat."

"Well, you must've heard wrong."

"It wasn't a coin, was it, old girl?" Spike said. "He gave you that lovely silver bell."

"Of course!" cried Isadore. "Thank you, Spike! He made it into a silver cat bell—the perfect way to hide it from me! Someone take it off her."

"NO!" shrieked Demerara. "THAT SILVER BELL BELONGS TO ME!"

Oz had never seen her so furious.

"You'd better do as he says," Lily said softly, stroking Demerara's neck. "I don't think he can do his spell without it."

"POOH to his stupid spell!"

"It's not a stupid spell—look, I don't know what it is any more than you do. But I can feel how important this is. Please let me give it to him."

"Well, I suppose if it's for you and Oz," Demerara said grumpily.

"Thanks," Oz said.

Lily undid the cat's purple collar and carefully removed the silver bell—which was unusually heavy for a cat bell, she noticed now—and gave it to Isadore.

"It's warm, but not burning me." He held it in his palm. "I haven't a clue how to turn this thing back into a coin. Did Pierre ever tell you how to read the writing on it?"

"I'd like to remind you that I'm a cat," Demerara said coldly. "Reading is not my strong point."

"I saw him do it once," Spike piped up. "We were in the workshop—before you made me immortal—and he accidentally dropped a pan on me. Well, we were friends by then, and Mr. Pierre burst into tears. 'My dear little pal,' he says, 'it's all over for you now—and I just can't bear it! Mother wouldn't like it, but I'll never forgive myself if I don't try!' And then he put a coin on the table and a candle behind it. And the next thing I knew I was as fit as a fiddle."

"Good grief," Isadore said. "He made Mother's special recipe for a lab rat!"

"He was ever so pleased with himself," Spike chuckled. "He said my strength was as the strength of ten, because my heart was pure. I think that's from a poem."

"But how did he read the wretched writing? It's going to be even harder now that it's on the inside of this bell!" Holding up Dad's trousers with one hand and clutching the silver bell with the other, Isadore hurried down to the workshop.

They ran downstairs after him—even Spike, who loved TV. In the workshop, Isadore found a candle in a candlestick.

"Where did he put it, Spike?"

"On that little table beside the wall," Spike said. "I was lying in the sink—there was blood everywhere."

"There's no need to be disgusting!" spat Demerara, watching her bell with jealous green eyes. Isadore laid it on the flat stone in the middle of the room. He took a small pair of pliers from the tool rack and pulled the silver bell apart until it was almost flat, though not coin-shaped.

Isadore placed the bell on the table, and the lighted candle behind it.

Nothing happened.

"Well, there you are," Demerara said. "You've ruined my bell. I hope you're satisfied."

Oz was bitterly disappointed; this recipe was the key to Isadore's magic chocolate. If he didn't find out how to make it, that picture of the future would never be changed.

"I'll ask the department to find me a powerful micro-scope," Isadore said. "I do think my brothers might have been a bit more helpful!"

"Can't you see it?" Lily was surprised. Everyone looked at her.

"See what?" Oz asked.

She pointed at the blank white wall. "The writing."

There was a silence. Isadore's mouth hung open. "Writing?" he whispered.

"And lots of numbers—come on, Oz!"

"I can't see anything except the wall," Oz said—a little uneasily, because it was spooky that Lily could see something invisible.

"But this is incredible," Isadore said. "Lily, my dear child, your gift is greater than I suspected!"

"Greater than YOURS," Demerara said, with a cattish snigger.

Isadore ignored her. "Pen! Someone get me a pen! And a piece of paper!"

Oz ran to the kitchen and found a pen and the back of an envelope. Isadore snatched them eagerly. "Right, Lily—start reading."

Lily's freckled face was pale and unhappy. "It's all jumbled up—I can't tell what's an 'a' and what's an 's'—"

Oz's heart sank again. Great, he thought—the only one who can see the writing, and she's dyslexic.

"Take your time, my dear," Isadore said softly. "You know a lot more than you think."

He was suddenly very calm and patient; Oz was a

little surprised to see what a good teacher he could be. One by one he coaxed each letter and number out of Lily, so that she stopped stammering and panicking and became more confident.

"I think this row says 30—X—c8634—but it doesn't make sense."

"Don't worry about that; it's making perfect sense to me. The numbers stand for Mother's magicalized cacao beans." Isadore glanced up from his scribbling and gave her a friendly smile that made his waxy face years younger. "We can start tomorrow—thanks to you!"

"Are you sure?" Lily was relieved; Oz could see how delighted she was to have done it. "What if I've messed up the spell by reading the wrong things?"

"My dear child, you've given me more than enough information—only I can mess it up now." Isadore waved the scribble-covered envelope triumphantly. "When this business is all over, I shall be delighted to give you the proper, academic lessons your parents have been paying me for—if I have time. As I said to Daisy, it's nothing to do with magic, and everything to do with using the intelligence you were born with."

Oz asked, "What do you mean, if you have time?"

"Oh, let's not worry about that," Isadore said. "We have far more important things to do—let the chocolate making commence!"

24

Chocolate Interrupted

The man known as J sat at a long table at the back of the empty cafe in Skittle Street, sipping a cup of tea, looking out of place in his immaculate dark gray suit among the plastic chairs and colored pictures of eggs and chips.

"I'm at a crucial stage in my work," Isadore said. "I'm just about to light the charcoal and select the cacao beans. We can't spare much time."

"I'm afraid you'll have to," said J. "Sit down."

Isadore, Caydon and the twins sat down at the table; Alan—who had appeared at the workshop to summon them all—went to the counter to fetch tea and juice.

J put a newspaper down on the table.

Oz read the headline for Lily. " 'Coffee Terror on Motorway 4.' " He didn't see why this had anything to do with them.

" 'A convoy of trucks carrying a hundred tons of coffee beans was held up on the motorway by masked thieves,' " J read. " 'The attack had all the hallmarks of the Schmertz Gang.' " He looked sternly at Isadore. "If you know anything about this—"

"I know absolutely nothing about it," Isadore said. "I have no idea what those maniacs want with a hundred tons of coffee."

Lily gasped suddenly. "Unless they're working for goblins."

"Yes, the goblins in the tube," Caydon said. "They love coffee."

Oz had heard all about the goblins, but couldn't see what they had to do with the gang.

J nodded grimly. "We know that goblins will do anything for coffee. It seems the Schmertz Gang have found that out too."

"But they'd have to be magic to do that," Lily said.

"We think one of them was magic enough to be able to see a goblin when he or she followed Isadore to his hideout."

"My magic fudge was mainly designed to keep the goblins away," said Isadore. "The rats were an easy matter— but those malicious little beasts were an utter plague when I first moved into my grotto. Every time I made a cup of coffee they'd come streaming out of nowhere!"

Isadore was very energetic today, but Oz thought he looked a little older than usual—there were wrinkles around his eyes, and a few gray hairs around his temples. Maybe this was a side effect of getting sober.

"Let's assume," J said, "that those goblins are working for the gang. The stolen coffee is their payment for doing something. At first we were afraid they'd planted a bomb deep in the London Underground, but Joyce and her London Transport police have combed every inch of the entire system. We then turned our attention to other places with goblin trouble."

"There are goblins in other places?" Oz was hardened to weird things by now, but still found it difficult to take goblins seriously—it was like taking garden gnomes seriously.

"All kinds of places," said J. "For instance, the BBC is riddled with them—who do you think wrecked their garden in 1983? But we're concentrating on the place where the gang can do the most damage—Heathrow Airport."

"Oh, crikey," Isadore said.

"Precisely. Our agent at Heathrow reported a strong smell of coffee in one of the heating ducts. Unless we can find out what the goblins did to get it, hundreds of innocent people could die."

They were all silent. Without looking at each other, Oz and Lily knew that the other voice was quivering between them, filled with fear.

"The prime minister doesn't like it." J was very grave. "Neither do I—this operation won't be any place for children. But we need you three for your detecting powers. It's a very serious matter, and I'll quite understand if you'd rather not get involved."

Oz's mouth was dry. In his official way, J was warning them that they might be hurt, or even killed.

"I'll do it," Lily said. "I can't pretend I'm not scared—but I'm more scared to think about all those people getting killed."

"Me too," Caydon said. "Imagine how we'd feel every time we heard about the bomb and we knew we could've done something."

"Me too," Oz said quickly, a little annoyed that the others had got in first with being brave.

J managed a smile. "Thank you all very much."

"What'll you tell our parents if we die?" Caydon asked.

"Good grief, Caydon," Isadore said, "you do have a talent for asking uncomfortable questions—you remind me of my ex-wife."

"A freak balloon accident, if you must know," J said, looking pained. "But nobody's going to die. Alan will be with you, and also an SMU agent from the bomb squad."

"Cool!" Caydon's eyes sparkled with excitement. "I've never seen a bomb."

"This is Rosie," Alan said. "She's the SMU operative in the bomb squad."

Rosie was a pretty young woman with short brown hair. She was holding a large brown and white springer spaniel on a leash. "Hi, everyone; this is Norris. He's here to sniff out any bombs while you three are sniffing out the magic."

Alan had driven them to Heathrow Airport. It was the height of the tourist season, and they had to wind through crowds of vacationers and piles of luggage to the SMU office behind the green line at Customs. They had all put on white anti-goblin suits and Alan had made them take a couple of test sprays of the anti-goblin spray, to make sure they could act quickly if they had to.

Lily bent to stroke Norris's smooth round head, thinking he was very sweet; she had expected a police dog to be big and fierce. "Is he magic?"

"No," said Rosie. "He's just a normal but very talented sniffer dog. He won't be scared by a few goblins—and neither will I."

"Rosie was recruited by the SMU when she caught a load of them in the control tower," Alan said. His blond head turned scarlet. "As a matter of fact, we're engaged."

"Congratulations," Lily said.

"We met at the SMU Christmas party," Rosie said, smiling at Alan. "That's quite a weird occasion—you have to make sure you're not being chatted up by a ghost!"

"And some of the old ones take their heads off when it gets hot," Alan added.

"Will you invite any ghosts to your wedding?" Caydon asked. "Can we come?"

Rosie laughed. "You can come, but we don't want to frighten our families—maybe we'll hold a private party for all our unexplained friends."

The door of the office opened. A man came in, wearing the uniform of an airport security guard. He was plump and pale, with a short fuzz of red hair.

"Hi, sorry I'm late." He held out an SMU card. "Kyle Wickes."

"You must be the guy who smelled the coffee," Alan said.

Kyle was staring at Oz, Lily and Caydon. "They're just kids! Nobody told me they'd be this young!"

"They've never met any goblins," Alan said, flashing a grin at the three children. "But I think it's fair to say they've had plenty of experience. You'd better put on some protective clothing."

"Oh—right." Kyle looked nervous, Lily thought; his hands shook as he pulled on the white anti-goblin suit; if he was this nervous before they'd even seen anything, why had he been recruited by the SMU?

She decided to stick close to Caydon. He was still treating everything as an adventure, which was irritating, but his high spirits were very encouraging—no matter what happened, he was determined to have a good time.

Using unmarked exits and hidden doors, Kyle led the way out of the airport building onto a huge stretch of tarmac. The air smelled of aviation fuel and there was a continuous roar of planes taking off and landing. "Over there is the hangar where the unexplained coffee smell was reported this morning; we'd better start there."

He set off across the ocean of tarmac toward the nearest aircraft hangar: a vast shed the size of several cathedrals. Lily felt a little silly walking behind him in her white suit, brandishing her can of goblin spray, and was glad nobody was around to see them.

"Ow!" Kyle squeaked suddenly. "Someone touched me!"

They all stopped in the middle of the tarmac. Norris the sniffer dog quietly sat down.

"Get a grip, mate," said Alan. "There's nobody else around for miles!"

"I tell you someone touched my ear!"

"It must've been the wind," Rosie said. "The air currents do funny things in these big spaces."

"I—I suppose so." Kyle swallowed.

They started walking again.

"Ow! That wasn't the wind!" Kyle's plump cheeks were pale and sweaty. "Someone just pinched my bum!"

Caydon and Oz snorted with laughter.

"Nobody's anywhere near your bum," Alan said. "Calm down."

"Sorry—" Kyle took a few deep breaths. "My imagination must be playing tricks on me."

"I'm surprised they let you in the SMU," Alan said. "They don't like us having imaginations."

Norris let out a sharp yelp.

"What's up with you?" Rosie gently tugged his leash.

They were entering the great hangar, where huge passenger jets loomed in the half-light. As she walked inside, Lily had a sense of something large moving behind her. She glanced quickly over her shoulder and saw nothing. Don't be silly, she told herself—but she edged closer to Caydon.

"OK," Alan said. "Where's this coffee smell, then?"

Kyle took something from inside his white suit. "Go and stand by the wall."

"What?"

He was holding a gun. "Get by the wall, I said!" His face was white as a sheet and his hands trembled; he took a step back and pointed the gun at them. "Do as you're told!"

Lily couldn't help crying out. Rosie grabbed her arm and pulled her to the wall. They stood together in a pale huddle with their hands up.

"You're working for the other side," Alan said quietly.

"But it's not too late to change your mind—put the gun down."

"It is too late," another voice said. "You've walked straight into our trap!"

Lily turned her head to see a man in a black leather jacket and a black balaclava that covered his face. He was also holding a gun.

"Isadore Spoffard betrayed us," the man said. "Thanks to him, my brother is dead and my wife is in prison. Thanks to him our plans were ruined. This time nothing's going to stop us. Wickes—kill them!"

"NO!" yelled Alan.

Frozen with fear, Lily gaped at the traitor Kyle. He raised the gun in his trembling hand—and it suddenly flew across the hangar.

"What was that?" the other man screamed, looking around wildly. "AARRGH!"

Some powerful force whacked the gun out of his hand and he screamed again as he felt his feet lifting off the floor. He rose into the air and was then roughly dropped to the ground. Kyle dropped like a ninepin beside him. The two men lay sprawled on the concrete, absolutely still and weirdly flat, as if something very heavy was holding them down.

There was a long silence.

"I don't understand," Rosie whispered. "What—what did that?"

Lily heard a huffing noise and suddenly remembered the day on Hampstead Heath. "It's EDWIN!"

Forgetting the danger, she ran joyfully toward the flattened terrorists and blindly felt for the invisible ghost elephant who was sitting on them. His skin was wrinkled and leathery; she could smell his dusty, faintly zoo-like smell, and he was wonderfully solid when she flung her arms around him.

"Edwin? I don't believe it!" Alan started laughing. "Well, I'm certainly glad he's taken a fancy to you kids—he appeared because he wanted to play!"

"It was Edwin who pinched Kyle's bum!" Caydon ran over to hug him. "Good for you, mate!"

"And then he saw the guns and saved our lives!" Lily was so happy she was almost crying. "Thanks, Edwin—you're the greatest elephant in the world!"

"Are those guys dead?" Oz asked. He hadn't met the ghost elephant, and was transfixed by the sight of Lily and Caydon hugging empty air.

"Probably just badly squashed," Alan said cheerfully. "I'll tell the backup squad to bring an ambulance."

Norris the dog was alarmed by Edwin and tried to hide behind Rosie. Oz went over to Lily, and was thrilled to pat Edwin's leathery invisible skin. Something like a gentle hand tickled his neck.

"That's his trunk," Lily said. "He's pleased to meet you."

Edwin left—so suddenly that Caydon nearly fell on

the squashed terrorist. Luckily the two men were still unconscious. Alan handcuffed them and called on his radio for help while Rosie picked up the two guns and put them in large plastic evidence bags.

"Phew," Lily said. "I'm glad we didn't die in a freak ballooning accident after all."

"Alan!" Rosie called sharply from across the hangar. "There's a real stench of coffee over here—Norris! Down, boy!"

The hangar echoed with Norris's angry barks.

Alan ran over; the twins and Caydon stopped thinking about Edwin and scrambled for the cans of anti-goblin spray they had dropped during the attack.

Rosie and Norris stood in the shadow of an enormous passenger jet. Norris was barking himself into a frenzy, and Rosie had to hold his collar with both hands to stop him from bolting away. The smell of coffee was so intense it made them all feel light-headed.

A sharp screech rang out through the gloom. Something black scuttled out of the cockpit window and dropped to the floor at Lily's feet.

For one second they stood gaping at each other; the creature was about twenty centimeters tall and looked like a cross between a bird, a bat, a lizard and a human. It was black all over, with huge transparent ears, long scraggy limbs and a hideous face with an expression of wicked stupidity.

Three more goblins flopped down beside it.

"SPRAY!" shouted Alan, pointing his aerosol.

Lily was rooted to the ground but Caydon and Oz managed to use their cans; the goblins hissed and scattered, vanishing like mist.

Norris wrestled out of Rosie's grip and shot across the hangar after them.

"Norris! Heel!"

The dog trotted back with something limp and black hanging in his jaws—Lily caught one glimpse of the dead goblin and looked away, shivering.

"Good boy." Rosie patted him, gently removed the withered, scaly goblin corpse from Norris's mouth and put it in an evidence bag. "Alan, get the kids out of here—they've been planting explosives—this is a job for the bomb squad now."

"OK, let's get a cup of tea," Alan said. "Or hot chocolate—anything but coffee!"

This made them all laugh and Lily's knees felt less wobbly. Outside the hangar, three black vans were racing across the tarmac.

"Goblins can plant bombs in very tricky places," Alan told them. "But the bomb squad knows where to look now. Thanks to a dead elephant, we've foiled the gang's plot. I might get promoted for this."

25

Three Chocolatiers

When they got back to Skittle Street, Mum and Dad were not there.

"I'm afraid they're at the hospital," Isadore told them.

Lily gasped. "Has the baby been born?"

"No, there's no sign of the baby yet," Isadore said. "But your mother has to stay in the hospital while they monitor her blood pressure and the baby's heartbeat—nothing serious, they just want to be safe. I said I'd stay here to keep an eye on you two."

"Can we go and see her?" Lily asked.

"Sorry." Isadore shook his head. "You're needed here—we haven't a minute to lose."

"Is there—is there still a chance?" Oz remembered the terrible vision, and the whole world stood still.

Isadore put his hand on Oz's shoulder. "It's today—one of the witches at the safe house told me the date. It will happen today—unless we can change the picture."

"What picture?" Caydon asked.

Lily didn't need to know the answer. "What do we have to do?"

"Today lasts until midnight," Isadore said. "We have until midnight to make my redeeming chocolate." There were streaks of gray in his dark hair, and gray speckles in his thin black mustache. "I had meant to give you all at least a week of special training—if you'd been my apprentices you wouldn't even have touched a cacao bean for your first three months. But we don't have that luxury. It's now half past four in the afternoon, which gives us seven and a half hours to make the greatest chocolate of my entire career. And I can't do it without you three."

"Will it be enough time?" Lily asked fearfully. "What if we mess it up?"

Isadore gave her an encouraging smile. "I wasn't lying to your father when I said I was an excellent teacher; Mother always said I was the best at training apprentices. You three are going to be my fast-track apprentices—by the time this night is over, you'll be real chocolatiers."

Under his instructions, Oz, Lily and Caydon crowded round the kitchen sink to wash their hands.

Caydon muttered, "Is it me, or does he look older?"

"I thought I was imagining it at first," Oz said, "but Uncle Isadore definitely does look a lot more wrinkled than he did this morning—do you think his immortality's wearing out?"

Lily dried her hands vigorously. "Let's hope it doesn't wear out before we've finished."

In the workshop a charcoal fire glowed red-hot in the fireplace. There was a big pan of raw cacao beans roasting slowly over the flames. Demerara—dressed in a little white apron and starched cap—stood on a chair on her hind legs, stirring the beans with a wooden spoon she held in her mouth. Spike stood on her head, holding his wooden spoon in his front paws (he was also wearing a tiny white apron and cap, which made the rest of him look even dirtier).

"Put these on, please." Isadore handed them white lab coats and starched white caps. "Oz, take over from the animals and stir the cacao beans slowly. Caydon, take a piece of burning charcoal and start another small blaze in the grate underneath the chocolate stone. Spike and Demerara, go inside the separator and oil the tray. Lily, take this silk cloth and polish up the three molds until they GLEAM!"

It felt good to be doing something and the children and animals threw themselves into their work. The workshop filled with the smell of slightly burnt chocolate cake. Spike and Demerara went inside the metal tank in the corner. Isadore pored over his mother's moldy notebooks, muttering to himself feverishly, as if learning something for an exam.

When the beans were roasted, they were poured

into the oiled metal tray in the separator. Banging the door shut, Isadore pulled a metal lever and the cylinder began to shake.

"The shell of the roasted bean must be separated from the inside, which is known as the nib—the part that makes the chocolate. Modern chocolatiers are too brutal at this stage; the Spoffard separator merely loosens the husk, which is then removed by hand." He sighed and glanced at his watch. "It's fiddly work, but it mustn't be hurried."

The shelling was extremely tedious and made their fingernails sore; each nib had to be coaxed out of its husk. They all sat around in near silence, intent on processing a heap of cacao beans that never seemed to get any smaller. Demerara and Spike helped, using their claws and teeth; the bossy cat had worked furiously without a single word of complaint—though she did mutter crossly when Isadore described her and Spike as "the animals."

At last the shelling was finished and the dusky nibs filled a deep silver bowl. On the table beside the wall Isadore laid out his mother's notebooks, a collection of tiny glass bottles with silver stoppers and various squares of the chocolate they had taken from Pierre's safe and the SMU vault.

"Pick up the molds in your right hands." Isadore looked tired and haggard, but his eyes burned. "Pierre's sun for Lily, Marcel's star for Caydon—and Oz, I think you are the true inheritor of my moon. When you use it, only good things will happen."

He tipped the cacao nibs onto the stone, warmed by the fire Caydon had built underneath it. Taking a knife with a round silver blade, Isadore crushed the nibs into crumbs, which slowly melted together into one glorious smooth, glossy, gloopy mass. Though they were in such a hurry, Lily found herself mesmerized by the skill of Isadore's bony fingers.

"Now the real magic begins." He scooped the melted cacao back into the silver bowl and gave each of the children a long golden spoon. "Stir the mixture, and keep a tight hold on those molds—I had to trick Pierre and Marcel into doing this when I first made my immortality chocolate. They thought we were making a cure for indigestion."

The three of them stood around the bowl, stirring the chocolate and clutching the golden molds.

"Ten o'clock!" muttered Isadore. "Here we go!"

He began to rattle out words, too fast for Lily to make anything out—and the mold was growing so hot and heavy in her hand that it was hard to think about anything else.

Every few minutes, Isadore called out a series of numbers and gave one of the tiny bottles to Spike or Demerara. The two animals shook a single drop from each bottle into the chocolate and each drop filled the room with a different smell—roses, violets, marzipan, cinnamon, vanilla, golden syrup and dark brown sugar. The melted chocolate in the bowl became more and more fragrant.

"Goodness, this takes me back," Demerara sighed. "We used to do this for Pierre—Spike, do you remember when you fell in with a whole bottle of 11256?"

"Do I ever!" chuckled Spike. "It was while he was working on that slimming chocolate—I swear I farted for two solid days!"

"Poor old Pierre," Isadore said. "It's possible to make immortality chocolate, but slimming chocolate was simply too good to be true."

The time was creeping on. Isadore—with beads of sweat breaking out on his forehead—told them to stop stirring the mixture and poured in a carton of thick cream. Lily hoped they were finished now, but it only seemed to be the start of another complicated process. Isadore told them to hold the golden molds on the table while he poured in the melted chocolate. Once again she felt the weird energy joining her to the other two and pulsing through her—just as she had felt it in the sunken tram.

"Ten past eleven!" groaned Oz. "How much longer is this going to take?"

"Have faith, dear boy—I must say the incantations—

I'm babbling as fast as I can." Isadore was haggard now, with hollow cheeks and deep wrinkles around his eyes.

The chocolate in the three golden molds had quickly set. Isadore turned them out on the table. They all stared in silence at the three beautiful medallions of perfect chocolate. The detail of each chocolate face was exquisite. The smile on the plump face of the sun was filled with joy. The smiling face of the star was romantic and dreamy. The stern face of the moon had a gentle wisdom.

"My masterpieces," whispered Isadore. "I'm glad I lived to see this sight one more time!"

He picked up a small silver hammer, and smashed the perfect chocolate into tiny pieces.

They were all horrified—the beautiful pieces of chocolate that had taken so many hours to make.

"What?" gasped Lily. "Why did you do that?"

"You haven't changed sides again, have you?" Oz asked.

"Trust me; it's all part of the process." Isadore swept the fragments of chocolate into another silver bowl. He placed the bowl on the chocolate stone and the three children watched in amazement as he seemed to stir it away into nothing.

Finally, his arm became still. He bent over the silver bowl, limp with exhaustion. All they were left with was one tiny disc.

"What a letdown," Caydon said crossly. "I've seen bigger chocolate buttons!"

"It's twenty to midnight," Oz said. "We'll never get to the Whittington in twenty minutes."

"Yes we can," Caydon said. "I'll fetch my mum and she can drive us."

Isadore stood upright. "That would take far too long." He placed the disc of chocolate in a glass tube, corking up the end carefully. "Come with me."

"I wish I knew what was going on," Caydon complained. "Why are we in such a hurry?"

"My dear Caydon, I admire your habit of asking awkward questions," Isadore said. "It's one of your finest qualities—but right now it's getting in the way." He swept open the door and shooed them out of the room.

"Good luck!" Spike called after them.

"Take care!" mewed Demerara.

Oz was so sick with worry he could hardly get words out. "What—? How—?"

"We could take a minicab," offered Lily. "There's an office round the corner."

"There's nothing else for it." Isadore was grim. "Please, children—don't get killed or I'll never be redeemed—we'll have to fly."

"Wow!" cried Caydon, his face lighting up. "Actually FLY, like Superman?"

"No, not at all like Superman—he didn't run the risk

of plummeting out of the sky. Link arms and hold on for dear life!"

Lily linked arms with Isadore on one side and Oz on the other; this was incredibly scary, but it was also like a dream, and she was painfully aware of the other voice calling in a plaintive way, like a bird moving away to the next valley.

She screwed her eyes tight shut; the pavement of Skittle Street dropped away from under her feet and the night air rushed around her face.

"This is AWESOME!" yelled Caydon.

"INCREDIBLE!" shouted Oz.

She couldn't help opening her eyes. They were shooting over the dark streets of Holloway, just above the level of the tallest houses, so fast that the long necklaces of street lights below were a blur. The Whittington Hospital was near the Archway branch of McDonald's, only a short distance from Skittle Street if you didn't have to bother with roads and traffic lights. Lily watched the ground rushing past underneath until the jumble of hospital buildings rose up to meet them—and suddenly they were all sprawled in a heap on the tarmac outside the emergency room.

"Ten minutes!" Isadore panted, struggling to his feet. He gazed around at the dozens of signs pointing to different departments. "X-Ray—Podiatry—Hematology— this place is enormous! Where do they keep the babies?"

"I know where," Caydon said. "My gran's one of the midwives—come on."

He hurried them to the end of the main building, to a small door with a notice: "Maternity Night Bell." It had a keypad and Caydon punched in the code.

It was a very good thing Caydon knew his way around; the place was a maze of sudden staircases and endless corridors. Very out of breath, they reached the Maternity Unit with six minutes to spare. Everything was very quiet, except for the machines bleeping and one baby crying a long way off.

Caydon put a finger to his lips. "Shhh! If my gran sees us she'll go crazy—I wish my shoes didn't squeak!"

He led them through a pair of doors marked "Prenatal Ward."

Lily looked into a side room with a glass door and her heart leapt. Dad was sleeping in a plastic chair, while Mum lay on a high bed with wires coming out of her and a large machine bleeping beside her. They crept into the room.

"She's asleep!" Oz moaned breathlessly. "How do we give her the chocolate?"

Isadore took the glass tube from his pocket and pulled out the cork. The small, hot room was suddenly filled with a beautiful smell of chocolate. "I'll just slip it into her mouth."

The door slammed open; an angry voice snapped,

"What do you think you're doing?" A stout black lady in a blue midwife's dress was in the room with them, standing between Mum and Isadore. "Are you trying to choke her?"

"Gran!" squeaked Caydon.

Isadore's mouth fell open with shock; he nearly dropped the disc of magic chocolate. "Elvira!"

26

Departure

"Give that to me!" Elvira snatched the chocolate from Isadore. "What took you so long?" She put the chocolate in the palm of her hand, blew on it and held it under Mum's nose, where it turned to mist and disappeared. In her sleep, Mum sighed and smiled. "She's taken it now—with just one and a half minutes to spare." Dad stirred in his chair, then seemed to sleep more peacefully.

"We did it!" Isadore collapsed into the plastic chair next to Dad. "Elvira, thank you."

"Gran?" Caydon was bewildered. "What's going on? Do you know him?"

"Oh, I know Isadore Spoffard," Elvira said. "I used to be married to him."

"WHAT!"

"Out of this room, everybody—these two tired parents need their sleep." The stern midwife suddenly smiled at Oz. "It's OK now."

"Really?" The surge of relief and hope took Oz's

breath away; it was like a great weight lifting off him. He knew Lily could feel it too. She took his hand as they went back into the corridor, and the other voice shot through them both in a pulse of the purest happiness.

Caydon was too astonished to pay attention to anyone but his grandmother. "You were married to Isadore?"

"I'm afraid so," Elvira said briskly. "Back when I was a silly girl in Jamaica."

"But—does Mum know?"

"Well, no." She was a little uncomfortable. "You see, when I came to England, I married your grandad, who wasn't a bit magic, and your mum takes after him. She didn't need to know about all that stuff."

"Hang on," Lily said. "Are you the local witch?"

"Yes, darling; I've been keeping an eye on Skittle Street for years, and Demerara reports to me—I wrote the letter that was supposed to come from the solicitor. The department wanted me to take on the whole mission, but I'm a working witch with a maternity unit to run, so I sent Caydon instead."

"But—but—am I magical, then?"

Elvira chuckled and patted his cheek. "Oh, you're as magical as they come—I could tell the minute you were born! I didn't mean to start training you till you were sixteen, but this was an emergency." She turned sharply to Isadore. "What will you do now?"

He looked very tired. "You know."

Her face softened. "I never thought I'd say this, but you did a very good thing today."

"I was merely making amends," said Isadore. "I've sent you back the deeds to your farm."

"Thanks, Isadore."

"Farm?" Caydon asked faintly.

"My family's farm in Jamaica; I'll tell you about it later."

"That's where I went with Isadore," Oz told him. "It's amazing."

"Wow—we have a farm!"

"Yes, but you three should be in bed," Elvira said. "Go right back to Skittle Street."

Caydon brightened. "Can we fly again?"

"You let them FLY?" Elvira turned furiously on Isadore. "My only grandson and these innocent twins? You could've KILLED them!"

"It was an emergency," he said quickly. "There wasn't any other way."

"Don't get mad, Gran." Caydon took Elvira's plump arm. "He couldn't help it, and we're fine."

"Hmmm," said Elvira. "Well, you can take the night bus home. There'll be no more flying, thank you very much!"

"Will you teach me flying when I'm sixteen? Will you teach me NOW?"

"Caydon Robert Campbell, stop pestering me while I'm at work. You'll learn magic when I'm good and ready—get home at once!"

Now that Oz had met Caydon's gran, he wasn't at all surprised to learn that she was a witch—when she was angry, her face was thunderous.

"I'll take good care of them," Isadore said quietly. "I'm glad we met again, Elvira. I'm sorry I cheated you all those years ago. The fact is, I wouldn't have married you if you hadn't been so beautiful."

"Oh, go on!" The fearsome midwife smiled, and was suddenly surprisingly young and pretty. "You could always talk the paint off a wall!"

"You won't see me again."

"I hope you find what you're looking for."

Oz caught the serious look that passed between them, and wondered what they were talking about.

"Thanks, Elvira." Isadore solemnly kissed her hand. "Thanks for everything."

"Excuse me," Lily said. "Do you know when our baby will be born?"

"Very soon." The local witch became businesslike again. "I hope you two are ready to be very helpful and change lots of nappies."

"Yeuch," Caydon said. "Yellow baby poo!"

"You cheeky boy—I'll deal with you when I finish my shift! Now get back home before I throw you there."

Caydon laughed and gave her a quick hug. "See you later."

"Nice to meet you," Oz said. The ridiculous happiness hadn't worn off, but he was starting to get worried about Isadore; he was stooping, and nearly all his hair was gray.

"You mustn't fret about him, darling," Elvira said gently. "He's going to be fine."

Isadore didn't seem fine. He had to cling to Oz's arm when they left the hospital and he was shuffling like a very old man. All three of them had to help him on and off the night bus. It took them ages to walk the short distance from the bus stop to Skittle Street.

"I'd better get to my house," Caydon said.

"We couldn't have managed without you, Caydon," Isadore said. "Thank you very much, and give my respects to your grandmother." It sounded to Oz as if he were saying goodbye, but Caydon didn't notice.

"OK," he said cheerfully. "Good night."

Isadore limped painfully into Number 18 and collapsed into a chair in the kitchen. When Oz switched the light on, he looked shockingly older.

"Uncle Isadore, are you OK?" Oz asked

"Never better, my dear boy. Perhaps you'd be kind enough to make me a cup of tea."

"Sure." Oz went to fill the kettle.

Lily yawned. "I feel like I've been up for days!"

"Go to bed," Isadore said. "There's nothing more to do now."

She looked at him properly. "You're getting older."

"A trick of the light! You must get some rest. But it's likely that I won't be here tomorrow morning."

"Oh," said Lily. "Where are you going?"

"That's not important. I just want to say how delightful it has been to know you, Lily, and I'm sorry I couldn't be your tutor. When you start your new school, don't let anyone accuse you of not trying, and don't accuse yourself of being stupid. Dyslexia is often a side effect of having magical gifts. Your brain is a very fine one."

"Thanks." Lily stared at him for a moment and then impulsively leaned forward and kissed his cheek. "Good night."

After she had gone, Isadore put a trembling hand up to his face. "She kissed me! I must already be redeemed."

Oz made him a mug of tea.

"You're exhausted, dear boy," Isadore said. "Maybe we should say our goodbyes now."

Oz sat down at the table. "I want to stay with you. Where are you going? You can tell me."

"I'm very happy, Oz—happier than I've ever been."

"Your immortality's worn off, hasn't it?"

"Yes." Isadore shakily took a sip of tea. "It was the one thing I had to give."

"What do you mean?"

"My life, dear boy."

Oz was silent for several long minutes. "You mean you're going to—die."

"Everyone dies, Oz," Isadore said firmly. "And I ought to have done it years ago. It's all part of the deal I struck with my brothers."

"Oh." Oz hung his head to hide the tears in his eyes.

"How kind of you to cry for me; I really don't deserve it."

"I'll miss you."

"And I'll miss you—if such a thing is possible where I'm going. My reformation is entirely due to you."

"Thanks for the violin."

Isadore smiled faintly. "I'm glad it's going to such a good home."

Oz had an idea. "Would you like me to play for you now?"

"I'd love it above all things."

Oz dashed up to his room to fetch Isadore's beautiful violin. He wasn't out of the room for more than a few minutes, but when he got back his great-great-uncle's mustache was white and his skin was like wrinkled tissue paper.

"Let's have the Mozart you played that first evening in my hideout. It makes me think of the orchard."

Oz played the Mozart while Isadore lay back in his

chair with a smile full of bliss. When it was finished, he played something else, and then something else. Tired as he was, Oz played and played, until the first signs of dawn began to streak the sky.

A shriek rang out above them. "OZ! OZ—where are you?" Lily was hurtling down the stairs. "Dad just called my phone—we've got a baby sister! She came very fast and she's totally perfect and weighs seven and a half pounds—and she's called DAISY!"

Isadore's eyes were closed. Oz touched his shoulder. "Did you hear that? Our baby's been born."

"Yes," whispered Isadore. "Daisy!" He tried to smile, but his eyelids fluttered and he lay still.

27

The Perfect Three

Lily—in her pajamas, with her hair standing out like mad—was in the doorway. "Dad's coming back for a shower and then we can see her—oh." She stopped and stared at Isadore.

"I think he's dead," Oz said, wiping his eyes. "I don't know what to do."

"So that's what he meant." Lily said. A deep silence settled as she gazed at Isadore, awed by his stillness and her brother's tears. A bird in the garden began to sing. "Maybe we should call an ambulance."

"That wouldn't be much use now."

"But we can't let Dad come back to a dead body!"

"I don't think that's going to be a problem," Oz said. Something strange was happening to Isadore. As they watched, what was left of his flesh withered away until he was nothing but a bunch of bones in a white suit. Lily ran to Oz and clutched his hand. The white suit then disintegrated and the bones crumbled. All that was left of Isadore Spoffard was a heap of pale ashes.

A breeze blew through the kitchen. The heap of ashes stirred. Oz shook off Lily's hand and ran to open the back door.

"What are you doing?" Lily asked.

The ashes lifted in a cloud and floated out into the garden. For a moment they hung there in the silvery summer dawn, and then a gust of wind blew them into nothing.

"I think I know where he's gone," Oz said. He hadn't told Lily about the three boys in the orchard, but in his mind's eye he had a glimpse of them under the trees, and he was sure the brothers were reunited at last.

The front door opened. "Oz! Lily!"

Dad was back from the hospital. He charged into the kitchen and hugged Oz and Lily so hard that their feet lifted off the ground. His face was pale and baggy and he hadn't shaved, but he was so happy that a wave of happiness seemed to sweep through the whole house.

"I'm so glad to see you both! It was pretty hairy and it all happened rather fast—but Caydon's gran was in charge and it went like magic! Your baby sister's gorgeous and I've taken a million photos but I think you should meet her in the flesh first." He released them. "Have you two been up all night? Where's Dr. Sneed?"

"You just missed him," Lily said. "When can we see Daisy?"

"I'll have a shower and you can get dressed," Dad

said. "And the cafe will be open by then—we'll treat ourselves to the biggest, unhealthiest breakfast in Holloway—and after that we'll go up to the hospital."

He dashed away upstairs.

Lily and Oz looked at each other.

"It's over, isn't it?" Lily said. "I feel a great calm in the marrow of my bones."

Upstairs, at the top of the house, a choir suddenly burst into song.

"*Daisy, Daisy, give me your answer, do;*
I'm half crazy, all for the love of you!"

The voices were high and sweet and piercing.

"It's those roses on your wallpaper," Demerara's voice said. "They've started a choir."

Lily dropped to the floor to hug and kiss the immortal cat. "I was scared you and Spike wouldn't be here anymore and I'd never see you again!"

"We'll always be here," Spike said, scuttling into the kitchen. "You can see us whenever you like."

"And you won't ever need to get a mortal cat now, because you've got me." Demerara was beaming, highly pleased with herself. "I'll be here whenever you or Oz or Daisy needs a sympathetic cat to talk to."

"Is our government work finished now?" Oz asked.

"Oh, yes," Spike said. "You and Caydon can make that Scalextric track; I like a bit of motor racing."

Oz was ridiculously light-hearted; after everything

they had been through, it was like flying, and he knew Lily felt it too. The feeling carried them through an enormous, fantastic breakfast at the Skittle Street cafe (the lady who owned it gave them all free tea and toast when she heard about Daisy) and back to the Whittington Hospital.

In a sunny ward, in which several new babies were squalling, they found Mum sitting up in bed with her arms out and ran to hug her.

A cross bleat came from the plastic box beside her bed.

Mum laughed softly. "Daisy wants to introduce herself."

"She likes to be the center of attention," Dad said.

Oz and Lily bent over the box. Their new sister was tiny and pink, with a fuzz of black hair, and a dab of a nose on her squashed face. She wore a little pink suit and snuffled like a cross hedgehog. Somehow, she fit into a space that had been waiting for her.

"Bruce, you'd better hand her back to me," Mum said, "before she starts bellowing."

Dad gently picked up the tiny, wriggling baby and put her in Mum's arms.

"You're all here now," Mum said. "I've never told you two this—but when I first got pregnant with you, I was expecting triplets, only I lost one." She smiled down into Daisy's face. "I was thrilled with my twins—but I never lost the nagging sense that someone was missing. And now I have my Perfect Three!"

Lily reached out and put her finger into the palm of Daisy's hand. "So Demerara was right after all—we were triplets! Now we can talk to her properly and she won't just be a feeling in our heads and you won't send us back to therapy."

"Good old Nutella," Dad laughed. "What are you going on about now?"

Oz understood. He put his finger into Daisy's other hand, and a pulse of understanding shot through the three of them—the Perfect Three, like the three boys in the orchard.

"You two have been fantastic," Mum said. "As soon as we're out of here, I have to think about getting all the things you'll need for your new school. I know you went to all those camps, but we haven't been away anywhere—I'm afraid you've had rather a boring holiday."

Oz and Lily looked at each other and burst out laughing.

"Oh, I don't know," Oz said. "It's had its moments." They laughed even harder—this had to be the understatement of the century.

"Oh, look," Dad said, "it's that young chap from the river police!"

Alan, very smart and red-faced in his uniform,

walked across the maternity ward carrying a huge bunch of pink roses.

"Hello, Alan," Mum said. "What lovely flowers—thank you so much."

"Congratulations," said Alan. "I've actually come to pick up Oz and Lily."

Oz was glad to see him—but what did the department want with them now?

Alan grinned. "It won't take long; it's just a small party for the end of the diving course."

The party, to Lily's delight, was at the unexplained kennels in Muswell Hill. The reception desk had been turned into a food table, laden with plates of sandwiches, cakes and cans of fancy cat food. Everyone they had met on their magical adventures was there—J, B62, the sergeant from the river police, the stewardess from Air Jamaica, Rosie from the bomb squad, Joyce from the London Transport police, Colonel Turnbull from the Tower—and of course Caydon and his gran.

"I just groaned when Alan came for me," Caydon told them. "I said, we've risked our lives and saved London from the gang—what more do you want? But Gran said it wasn't another job."

"You've met that nice new sister of yours," Elvira

said. "She'll keep you busy!" She sniffed suddenly. "What on earth is that smell?"

"Just a dab of disco body glitter," mewed Demerara. "Since my lovely curls were taken away. This is a very special occasion and I wanted to look my best in the photograph."

"I still think I look stupid," Spike said. His straggly fur was packed with glitter and he wore a pink bow around his neck.

"Nonsense, Spike—you merely look CIVILIZED," Demerara said loftily. "If I had my way, you'd have a proper BATH."

The glittering rat chuckled. "Hold on, old girl! I've given up smoking but rats don't have baths—none of my mates would recognize me!"

"Ow! Did you pinch me? How dare you!"

"I think that was Edwin," Lily said. "We're right by his cage." She put her hand through the bars and felt the soft, leathery touch of the invisible trunk. "Come and meet him properly, Oz—he's so sweet!"

Oz and Caydon came over to the empty cage to stroke the ghostly elephant, and were laughing at his tricks when J called for silence.

"Ladies and gentlemen, thanks to your hard work and bravery, this department has completed the most successful operation in its history. An evil genius has been defeated and a dangerous gang has been destroyed. The prime minister has instructed me to give out a number of awards. First, Demerara and Spike."

"Well I never," said Spike.

"An AWARD?" mewed Demerara. "How kind!"

B62 removed the pink bow from Spike's neck and replaced it with a tiny gold medal on a blue ribbon.

"Well done, Spike," J said. "You've done brilliant work on this operation."

"Wow—a medal! Me with a medal!" Spike's glittery whiskers bristled with joy. "Well I never!"

"I hope mine's a bit bigger," Demerara said.

"Don't worry, we haven't forgotten you," J said, smiling down at the immortal cat. "You haven't always been the easiest agent to work with—but we couldn't have done it without you. Instead of a medal, we decided to give you this new solid gold cat bell."

He held out a beautiful, gleaming bell. Demerara was so thunderstruck with happiness that for once she could hardly speak. "It's—oh, Lily—it's WONDERFUL—collar—put it on my—"

Lily knelt down to put the new bell on the cat's purple collar, and Elvira kindly held up her pocket mirror so that the two proud animals could see themselves.

Everyone clapped.

"Oz, Lily and Caydon," J said. "You three have been magnificent."

"Hear, hear!" shouted Spike.

Lily felt her face turning hot; everyone was looking at her.

"You'll be glad to hear," J said, "that you won't have any more duties with this department. When you're older you may find yourselves working for the SMU in some capacity or other—but for now you should be concentrating on normal, everyday things."

"Huh," Caydon muttered. "I was hoping we could get off school!"

"In your dreams," his gran snapped.

"But it's been so fantastic—I can't just go back to normal life!"

"I can't wait," Oz said. "I don't care if I never see anything weird again."

Lily squeezed his hand to show she felt the same; she loved the immortal animals, but that was as much magic as she wanted now.

"The prime minister wanted to give the three of you very special awards," J said. "Oz, all your music lessons with the best teachers will be paid for—your parents will believe you've won a scholarship."

"Wow, thanks." Oz often worried about the cost of his violin lessons; it was great to know that they would now be free.

"Lily," J said, "we're sending you one of our specialist SMU tutors; she's an expert in both dyslexia and magic."

Lily didn't want another tutor, but had to admit some help would be welcome; she had been getting nervous about the work at their new school. "Thanks."

"And Caydon, since you're so fond of adventures in the unexplained, you'll spend two weeks every summer with our special secret unit of SMU police cadets."

Caydon punched the air. "WICKED!"

"Finally," J said, "the PM wanted to do something nice for Edwin."

The room burst out into loud clapping and cheering; the old ghost elephant was very popular.

"It was tricky," J went on, "because ghosts don't want or need anything. We decided to get him this." He held up a large red beach ball. "Lily, please give this to Edwin with something he'll really like—a promise that you'll come and play with him sometimes."

"Oh—I'd love to!" Lily took the red ball. B62 opened Edwin's cage and she went inside. "Here you are, Edwin, and I'll pop in next Saturday if that's OK—I'll tell my dad I'm going to ballet."

The ball was gently knocked out of her hand and began to bounce on the floor and off the walls. Lily spent the rest of the party playing catch with an invisible elephant.

When even Demerara had had enough to eat, it was time to return to Skittle Street and (relatively) ordinary life.

"This has been the most incredible summer ever," said Caydon.

"Amazing," Oz agreed, with a mighty yawn.

Just as they were about to leave the kennels, B62 touched Lily's arm. "Look behind you," she whispered.

Lily looked over her shoulder, and for one glorious moment saw an elephant standing on his hind legs, twirling a red ball at the end of his trunk.

A moment later he was gone, leaving Lily dazzled.

I've seen Edwin, she thought. Oz is safe and Daisy's here, and I've actually seen Edwin; this is probably the happiest day of my life.

She walked out into the sunny morning with the choir of wallpaper roses singing inside her head.

I'd like to thank my helpful nephew Max for reading an early version of this book—and for sending me a great T-shirt that says "Old Fairies Rock" after reading my last book, *Magicalamity*.

The "old Italian novel" that Isadore mentions on page 199 really exists; it's called *The Betrothed* (*I Promessi Sposi*) by Alessandro Manzoni; if you want to freak out the grown-ups, request it for Christmas.

Kate Saunders has written lots of books for adults and children. She lives in London with her son and her three cats.